Head of the Lakes
Selected Short Stories

Head of the Lakes
Selected Short Stories

Anthony Bukoski

With a foreword
by Nick Hayes

NODIN PRESS

These short stories have been selected from the fifty-one stories in *Children of Strangers* (Southern Methodist University Press, 1993), *Polonaise* (SMU, 1999), *Time Between Trains* (SMU, 2003), and *North of the Port* (SMU, 2008). In 2011, Holy Cow! Press published *Time Between Trains* in paperback. Nick Hayes's foreword first appeared as "Superior's East End and Anthony Bukoski's Ghosts," an essay in *MinnPost*.

ISBN: 978-1-947237-06-3

Design: John Toren

Second printing

Cover and author photos: Diane Merchant, Morton Grove, Illinois.
Library of Congress Cataloging-in-Publication Data
Names: Bukoski, Anthony, author. | Hayes, Nick, 1947- writer of introduction. Title: Head of the lakes : selected short stories / by Anthony Bukoski ; with an introduction by Nick Hayes.

Description: Minneapolis, MN : Nodin Press, [2018] | "These short stories have been selected from the fifty-one stories in Children of Strangers (Southern Methodist University Press, 1993), Polonaise (SMU, 1999), Time Between Trains (SMU, 2003), and North of the Port (SMU, 2008). In 2011, Holy Cow! Press published Time Between Trains in paperback. Nick Hayes's introduction "Superior's East End and Anthony Bukoski's Ghosts" first appeared as an essay in MinnPost." -- ECIP galley.

Identifiers: LCCN 2018007486 | ISBN 9781947237063

Subjects: LCSH: Polish Americans--Fiction. | Blue collar workers--Fiction. | GSAFD: Short stories.

Classification: LCC PS3552.U399 A6 2018 | DDC 813/.54--dc23
LC record available at https://lccn.loc.gov/2018007486

Published by
Nodin Press
5114 Cedar Lake Road
Minneapolis, MN 55416
www.nodinpress.com

For John W. Groth (1944–2008)
Larkspur and Redwood Valley, California
Semper Fidelis

Acknowledgments

I am grateful to Kathryn M. Lang and Southern Methodist University Press for first bringing these stories to print in book form. I also want to thank Thomas Napierkowski, University of Colorado-Colorado Springs, my friend and mentor, for encouraging me to write about Polish Americans in northern Wisconsin. For forty-eight years, Elaine, my wife, has provided me time to write. For that, I am most grateful. I am also indebted to John Merchant, Loyola University of Chicago, and to Jo Mackiewicz, Iowa State University, for their encouragement and friendship.

CONTENTS

FOREWORD

I f your summer travel takes you to Duluth or the North Shore, hold off on the new cuisine restaurants, fancy wine bars, and brew pubs. As I-35 rolls into the Twin Ports, take a right onto the Bong Bridge and follow Highway 2 to Superior's East End. You'll find there the world of Anthony Bukoski's ghosts. "Ghosts like me stand on the street waiting for the old days when we were not ghosts," he once wrote in an essay for Wisconsin Public Radio's "Wisconsin Life" series.

Bukoski has done for Superior's East End what Raymond Carver did for the down-and-out of the Pacific Northwest or Pete Hamill did when annexing New York for the Irish. He's brought back to life Superior's Polish Americans and the blue-collar community from its boom days in the post-World War II era to its decline and near disappearance in recent times.

Bukoski describes a town and a neighborhood where there's plenty of emptiness to go around. A century and a half ago, whoever laid out the city grid made sure there'd be plenty of room for loneliness. The city limits encompass an area roughly equivalent in size (minus a square foot or two) to Minneapolis. Superiorites enjoy a lot more elbow room than the 383,000 of us who call Minneapolis home. The town loses any pretense of population density as you drive away from the shipyard and the worn downtown and follow East Second Street to Superior's East End, where deep setbacks separate one house from another and empty fields sometimes isolate one section of a neighborhood from the next.

To get to Superior, population 27,244, don't bother with

the tourist guidebooks. Some places are too lonely even for the *Lonely Planet*. Superior's official website will send you to the city's 36-hole golf course or to Barker's Island Marina. The State of Wisconsin omits the East End from its list of "tourist destinations." If you really want to travel here—and you should—don't call the Chamber of Commerce, forget about the Wisconsin Department of Tourism's tips, chuck the travel guidebooks, and let any of Bukoski's six short-story collections take you back to the lost world of a Polish-American community.

Bukoski's writing career started inauspiciously. As a student at what was then Wisconsin State University-Superior, he edited the student journal. "Even though I was editor," he recalls, "my stories were so bad that I rejected them." One of his early publications had been rejected 28 times. When it was accepted on the 29th try, the journal's editor sent him a $5 check with a note asking the author to please remit the money as payment for a subscription. Then Bukoski's luck changed. St. Paul-based New Rivers Press published his first book, *Twelve Below Zero,* in 1986. Between 1993 and 2008, Southern Methodist University Press published his next four books to good reviews in *Publishers Weekly, Kirkus Reviews,* and *Booklist*.

Not all of his characters are Polish American. Nor does every story take place in Superior. The city's East End is actually an ethnic mix of Swedes, Finns, Native Americans, and others. Never mind. "I've claimed it for Poland," Bukoski admits. In one story, as the winter wind from the lake punishes the streets, he describes four young men with nothing better to do than drink. One of their two bar tours takes them "around the horn," paying a call at Hudy's Polish Palace and other places. The more daunting "Death March" stops in at every bar along downtown's Tower Avenue.

Here the taverns have Happy Hour from 6 to 9:30 A.M. for those getting off of the night shift and 4 to 6:00 P.M. for those finishing the day shift. The music of Dr. Kielbasa, the

Wally Na Zdrowie Trio, and the World's Most Dangerous Polka Band rattles the walls of the Thaddeus Kosciuszko Lodge. A simple piety and spiritual comfort reside in the Church of St. Adalbert. At least things were once that way. The Chamber of Commerce, of course, would rather Bukoski got on-message with its upbeat branding. However, for Bukoski a disarming lack of pretense gives his beloved hometown its character.

We first met in a trendy Superior coffeehouse (my choice, not his) that appeals to a skinny, café latte crowd. Eyeing a bottle of Perrier, Bukoski said, "It's ridiculous to sell water like this in Superior." It takes more than Perrier to ease his characters' troubles. "Everyone living in the dirt and wind here," Bukoski writes in "Dry Spell" from *Polonaise*, "is left over or hungover—from a business that failed, from a marriage that failed, from a church that closed, from a drinking bout, from general unhappiness."

In "Report of the Guardian of the Sick" from *North of the Port*, the unhappiness of a father and son are heart-rending. In the story, Pete Dziedzic, a Marine, has returned from Vietnam (Bukoski, a former Marine, served in Vietnam) to resume an emotional and psychological war with his father. Al Dziedzic doesn't care if his son has been one of "the Few, the Proud, the Marines." As far as Al is concerned, a kid who can't clean a bathtub, who doesn't appreciate the Chmielewski Brothers polka band on TV, and who skips Mass at St. Adalbert's is a *dupa*.

Al doesn't tell his son that a lifetime of working in the flour mill has damaged his lungs. Let the *dupa* learn about it from his mother or from the Sick Director's report at the Polish Club. Outmatched, the son is resigned to stay with his father "until they both died of the wounds that had been inflicted over the past twenty years."

Not every Bukoski story brings tears. "Antoni Kosmatka Resists the Goddess of Love," also from *North of the Port*, begins, "The morning after he'd ogled the striptease dancer, Mr.

Kosmatka received a copy of the city's Shaming Ordinance." The story tries to keep a straight face as it follows the elderly Kosmatka's misguided pursuit of a dancer who performs in a Duluth striptease joint.

Polish Americans suffer many slights. The popular media joke about them. Polish-American writers are left out of the literary "canon" shaped by university elites. The Catholic Church in America has also sometimes treated its Polish faithful with condescension, embarking on its own "ethnic cleansing." The "ethnic parishes"—a code phrase for the urban Polish and East European Catholic churches—seem to be at the top of virtually every bishop's or diocese's list of parishes to close. For example, not long ago the Vatican questioned the appeal of Holy Cross Parish in Northeast Minneapolis to remain open. The heart of the city's Polish-Catholic community, Holy Cross is also a gem of religious architecture.

Bukoski has seen the Holy Cross story before. In 1981, the Diocese of Superior announced the closure of St. Adalbert's. Founded early in the century, the church, school, and rectory were landmarks standing at the intersection of 23rd Avenue East and East Third Street, claiming the East End for Poland.

Bukoski's father, who like the fictional Al Dziedzic worked at the flour mill and served on the parish council, appealed to the bishop in a letter. "Three generations of families have had their spiritual needs fulfilled in this little church which we cherish," it begins. "We respectfully reject the idea that national insularity alone is represented in churches such as ours." The writer's eloquence and piety should have convinced the bishop that St. Adalbert's was performing a much-needed service to Superior's other working-class ethnics. The bishop sent no reply.

The end came slowly. First, the school went, then the church. Thirty years later, a wrecking crew tore down the old rectory. The workers took their time, giving themselves a few weeks to rip off the clapboard siding piece by piece, next to demolish the frame and interior, and, finally, to reduce the pastor's home to a few dumpsters of trash consigned to a landfill. Standing on the sidewalk, an old-timer from the parish's better days watched and wept.

Today, not so much is left of Bukoski's old neighborhood, but there's enough to remember how it was. Thankfully, Hudy's is still open on East Fifth Street, a couple of blocks away from where St. Adalbert's stood.

Stop in for unhappy hour at the bar.

> *– Nick Hayes, Professor of History and*
> *University Chair in Critical Thinking,*
> *St. John's University, Collegeville, Minnesota*

The Tools of Ignorance

1. The Voices I Heard

I wipe beer glasses at the bar of Heartbreak Hotel in Superior. I turn the radio dial. I wonder where do the short, sweet seasons go to? Last year, I got free drinks and Shrimp-Buster sandwiches at Herby K's, got my muffler fixed free at Mufflers of Shreveport, got autograph requests all up and down Louisiana Avenue. That was before the bartender at Herby K's and the waiters at the Hayride Kitchen in Shreveport turned their backs on me. It is a story of loss and regret that has brought me home to northern Wisconsin.

Now who do I have to listen to but Pete Katzmarck in the corner of the bar staring at the hands of the Hamm's Beer clock? I tell him, "You're pickled. Go on home, you gaboosh, Pete."

"*You* go home, Augie," Pete says to me. "If I couldn't hit no better'n you, I'd never sign a contract. Bitter, bitter disappointment, *gorzki*."

"*Starość nieradość,*" this other guy, Władziu, moans in Polish. "Old age ain't any fun."

Somebody plugs in the jukebox. Eddie Blazonczyk's band comes on. Horns and accordions begin. On the phonograph, a guy yells:

Polka Time! Polka Time!
We're all fine at Polka Time!

I turn down the baseball game playing on the radio. Since it is growing dark, I flick on the switch to light the outdoor sign. Even the blue neon is heartbroken. Sizzling a little, only parts of the sign come on: HEARTBREAK OTEL.

I look in the mirror behind the bar. I see myself everywhere. Behind the bottle of *Jeżynowka* blackberry, it's me Augie, barkeep. Bum. Loser. I see me in Pete's face … in the old guy's faces slobbering over bowls of beer. Losers. Derelicts. Gabooshes.

"*You* go home!" Pete says.

"I've got nothing there but my ma waiting, Petie. What'll I do at home? I'm better off here. Either way I'm washed up. Jeezus, I threw my life away. I should've married this gal I knew down in Shreveport. What do I got now when I can't do nothing but think of her? I'm twenty-five. I'm through. No more baseball except what I play to embarrass myself on Sundays."

"You look like shit on Sundays," someone calls from the other end of the bar.

Over the cloudy jar of pickled pigs' feet, I stare in the mirror, wishing a storm would come to steam up the mirror and blow out the neon sign in front, so that I could serve the guys by flashlight or candlelight. Then you couldn't see our ceiling that's turned orange from seventy years of smoke or the mirror or the nicks in the long wood bar.

I've got to get a better job, or someday I'll be a washed-up geezer taking Pete's spot at the bar. I can't get over Shreveport, though. My heart's in Shreveport on the Red River because of what happened. Was it the night we returned from Jackson, Mississippi, and Ellie Pleasaunt was waiting at the players' entrance to the stadium? I got tangled up in something very serious in Shreveport that was partly the result of my foolishness and pride and partly my disregarding someone who loved me. It eats at me every night, so that when I look in the mirror behind the bar now and ask myself above the polkas and schottisches, "Did you *really* love her," the answer is still "yes" from my broken heart up north in Yankeeland.

Why I didn't listen to the Voice of the Shreveport Captains and keep from coming back to such a miserable place of heartbreak as the East End is a two-year history of bus trips, doubleheaders, and rain delays. In this, Augie Wyzinski's true-life chronicle of lost love, I'll get the record-book stuff over first. Like how in high school I lined a blue darter into the screen that protects the windows of a paper mill in Menasha, Wisconsin—430 feet into the wind off Lake Winnebago. Like how after the Oshkosh game in college, with the season I had my junior year, the Giants signed me. The *Evening Telegram* of my hometown here had on its front page: "LOCAL BOY SIGNS." My ma, Uncle Louie, and I couldn't finish our dinner at the Polish Hearth for all the commotion. The Duluth paper wanted an interview, too. Bennett Stodill, the sports editor, wouldn't let me touch my cabbage rolls. "You're going to make it. I know that," he said. My ma smiled, my uncle patted my shoulder. "See?" Ma said as the future lit up for me.

The Giants assigned me to Clinton, Iowa. I tore up the Midwest League—Cedar Rapids, Kane County, Burlington. Ma sent clippings: "FUTURE BRIGHT FOR SIGNEE WYZINSKI"…"BIG CLUB TO PROMOTE LOCAL TO AA AFTER FULL SEASON IN IOWA. FRISCO NEXT?"

I wasn't going to toil in the low minors long, I told myself.

From Clinton, the next season I went to Shreveport, Double-A. The first month there, April, I hit six homers, four doubles. After I tossed out my fifteenth base runner trying to steal, I couldn't walk into a clothing store or a nightclub on Louisiana Avenue without someone buying me a shirt or a drink just so they could be near me. You've heard of such phenoms as me.

Everything was great. ("Everytink great," the old gabooshes would say.) Things like this happen. Guys get lucky. I come out of college, I come out of northern Wisconsin. At the right moment, success and love strike me. Maybe no one from here will ever again catch on like this. Uncle Louie would talk about a "Hurricane" Bob Hazle that rose out of nowhere late one season in the '50s to help the Milwaukee Braves win a pennant. Then he was gone into oblivion like me. Now I'll explain how I, Augie, ended up at Heartbreak Hotel where the "bellhop's tears keep flowin'" and show why I, Augie, forgotten, oblivion-bound Augie, wear a baggy wool uniform these days on Sundays in Superior instead of the one with the orange and black SF of the big club, San Francisco. This is where the voice I should have listened to comes in. There were 50,000 watts of power behind that voice.

2. Giants' Signee Advertises Goody's Headache Powders

Who'd argue with 50,000 watts or question Biff Barton, the radio Voice of the Shreveport Captains? Mr. Barton had a full head of black hair he used Vitalis in. But in the front of his scalp, it was like you could see each individual strand where it grew out. His forehead and face were tanned. He wore tinted glasses that turned darker if the room or the press box was dark. Who'd argue with the power of his God-like voice? "Howdy, Louuu-eee-siana," he'd say over the airwaves with 50,000 watts to back him up.

He studied us, studied statistics, talked about us. "You know," Mr. Barton would say when I saw him at Shooter's Smokehouse Café in Shreveport, "it's a great game I hope you stick with, kid." I knew he had faith in me. He interviewed me on the field after a Tulsa game. "Those were king-sized homers last night," he said. "Your throwing arm is a rifle, too."

"I'm seeing the ball good, Mr. Barton," I said into the microphone as I looked at my reflection in his dark glasses.

"I'll say it's early in the season. Kid, you don't know your strength. You're soon going to be living on the West Coast. Fans in the Ark-La-Tex listening to this broadcast: Come out here to have a look-see. He's liable to be gone soon, called up to the big club."

"Keep your nose clean," he said to me afterward

"Don't worry," I said. "No smoking. No drinking."

In Tulsa, I threw out three more runners. I knocked in six runs in one game, five in another. In El Paso, I had a scorcher off the flagpole at Dudley Field. At Smith-Willis Stadium in Jackson, Miss., I got two doubles. Sportswriters called it a "meteoric" rise.

"Keeping my nose clean," I'd say when I saw Mr. Barton before games.

I kept on hitting and playing defense like the Milwaukee Braves' "Hurricane" Bob Hazle Uncle Louie told me about. June went by. "Everything was good then, wasn't it, Augie?" I ask myself in the mirror behind the bar now, recalling how I got four hits in a day game with San Antonio and the night that followed with Ellie, this woman who adored me. She was a lovesick fan. Before I met her, I was out every night after games pulling hijinks at the Sports Page in Shreve Square, at Mike and Lulu Longrie's Dugout Saloon on Line Ave., at The Cove on Cross Lake. So many women love a hard-hitting catcher that you can fill out different lineup cards every night. Once in a motel room after a twi-night doubleheader with Beaumont, a rookie named Denise, naked, wore my chest protector, crouched, and gave me the signal for fast ball. Another time in my apartment after a tight home game with Midland, I wore the catcher's mask through the whole act of "coytis." But one moonlit night after gunning down four baserunners and going two-for-three against the Arkansas Travelers, I got even luckier; I came home and pulled off a triple play with three gorgeous roommates who loved my swing. Then her, Ellie. She fell for me right away. We met at the Captains' Booster Club Pig Roast when I brought her a paper plate of coleslaw, pig meat, and Jo Jo's. Despite what sportswriters called my "furious pace," something was missing in my life like it was in Ellie's, I guess.

On the night I think of now, Ellie and I'd been going out a couple weeks. Her loneliness and the pressure on me of my sudden fame in the South, all of it—I don't know—came together that very night in the quiet of my apartment when we kissed each other. "I think I'm in like with you," I told her, looking into the shadows of her face. You don't say such things to women on the first date. But it was three weeks we'd been dating, and I could honestly tell her I liked her and partially commit myself to her—except for when I felt the urge to go on the prowl, drinking and looking for women who appreciated my star quality.

"I'm deeply in like with you, too, Augie," she said, looking up. "I'd give you my heart."

I buried myself in her neck and hair then.

The two of us lying there, I said her profile reminded me of a picture I'd seen of an ancient Egyptian queen, Never-Titty.

"I want you to feel like her husband," Ellie said.

"I wasn't alive back in ancient times before the designated hitter rule," I said.

"I was just teasing," she said. "I've been buried and you woke me and I'm in love. Nefertiti's in love." She moved a wisp of hair from her beautiful white forehead with the blue vein in her left temple. Like Never-Titty's, her nose had this very attractive bend. To me she was a goddess.

"We're not going to sleep tonight," I said, "but I'm sure happy and don't give a darn. Look-it the homers I got today."

After all this baseball stardom, then Nefertiti giving me her heart, regret and misfortune had to follow. It just seems like whenever I'm on a roll, I always do something dumb to mess up. Maybe it's part of my personality that I don't know how to hold on to the good things. Maybe I got what's called "low self-esteem." Now I have come to be counseled by winos and gabooshes with a really high regard for themselves who, when I say, "I ain't any good," they say, "You're right."

"But I once was, wasn't I, boys?" I ask.

"You no good ever. You were lousy. You stunk. We seen you play in the old-timers' baseball league on Sunday, too. You stink."

But once not so long ago, I was in Shreveport under blue Louisiana skies, and there I had a fine time and there I met a woman named Nefertiti. *When I look in the mirror, I still see her, heartbroken, looking back. When you said you'd give me your heart that night, Ellie, I looked in your eyes and said I would not hurt you, and later you carried my baby. On the night you gave me your love, I didn't know how much I would fail you. But I did fail you, Ellie Pleasaunt, because I could not accept your innocent love, because I did not have it in me.*

A MONTH AFTER THE TULSA interview, I was Biff's guest again— this time when he was promoting Goody's at Winn-Dixie Grocery. "Anybody who's had a headache," Biff Barton said over 71 KEEL-Radio, "get down to Jewella Avenue. Meet the Voice of the Shreveport Captains and Biff's very special interview guest today." While Ellie called her mother to say, "Turn on KEEL, quick!" Biff had me practice what he'd written on a scrap of paper. "Catching's hard work," I was saying nervously over the airwaves before I knew it. "When I get home with sore muscles, what do I reach for?" Here Mr. Barton held out the microphone. "GOODY'S!" the customers in Aisle 7 shouted.

Every night last summer, the Voice of the Shreveport Captains, the Old Testament God Biff Barton's voice, came over Big Thicket Country (as it does tonight when I'm working in a bar in Superior a thousand miles away). You'd look up through the smoke haze in the late innings at Beaumont, see him in the little square lighted press box, see him at V.J. Keefe Stadium in San Antone, at Windham in Little Rock, looking down through his tinted glasses at the way we carried ourselves. You'd pull into Marshall, Texas, and hear Mr. Biff, who influenced our manager's decisions. You might live on the bayou in

Homer, Louisiana, or be up in Helena, Arkansas, fixing your car, and you'd hear Biff's scouting report and interview show from down on the field. *Did you pass Ellie Pleasaunt on your road trips, Mr. Barton? Did you see her crying when she learned we were going to have a baby?*

3. Texas League Home Run King

My whole name is August Joseph Wyzinski. Old guys call me "Ow-goost." I was famous for a couple months, but I began wondering about my future when our manager, we called him the skipper, stopped looking me in the eye and benched me in Midland-Odessa in mid-July when I'd dropped a foul tip for strike three.

"Bet you'd go for a Polee sausage," the skipper'd say and spit tobacco. Sometimes pronouncing it "Pulley sausage," he'd ask on the field, "What you Yankees up north call that stuff you eat?"

"Kielbasa."

"Well, from now on you're Augie Kielbasa with them sausage hands that cain't hold onto a baseball."

"Pete, you spilled your beer," I say a year later. "Here's a bar rag. Wash your face while you're at it."

"You looking in mirror. What d'you know about my face?"

"I know. That's what I'm saying. I'll wipe *mine*, too."

Wipe my face with a bar rag because I've been a fool, Pete.

"Was I any good ever at anything, you guys?" I ask.

"No good. Right from the start, no good."

"Thanks."

"You welcome, Augie," Pete says.

"Ah, who wants a bowl of beer on me? Why not play me for a fool? I've thrown it all away. But what's the use of telling you gabooshes? Just remind me that I didn't deserve her and that I'm a fool. Tell me, Pete, was I a fool?"

"Sure, Augie."

"But why? I want to know."

"Because you are and you're no good with a baseball."

"Ah, you're right, Pete and you guys. That's what I don't understand about myself, how I can come so close to the good things and blow it every time. That's why I can't see any future for me. All I can do is think about the past. What kind of life is that to have?"

4. "Ow-Goost's" Night of Terror or How "Ow-Goost" Always Manages to Screw Things Up

One night last year we'd gone extra innings at home against the Beaumont Golden Gators, and though I hadn't caught, I was still tired. I'd been warming the bench, eating peanuts, thinking about my late nights with Ellie Pleasaunt and what I'd gotten into with her. I missed the night life—drinking, carousing, trading off of your fame to see how far you could get with a gal.

After Mr. Barton's stirring account of the game, KEEL-Radio had gone back to regular programming. Life was boring again. The parking lot was burning from sixteen hours of Caddo Parish heat when, all cleaned up, I came out of the clubhouse.

When you're famous and in a batting and fielding slump, you need something to cheer you up. You have a nice car from your signing bonus of a few years back and plenty of time after games. If you're short of dough, you fool gals who follow ballclubs by carrying a money clip with fifty bucks showing and a wad of dollar bills beneath it. A few of the Captains have girlfriends in the Texas League towns. I had Ellie since I'd settled down from the wild days of April in Shreveport when I was out every night with Linda, D.J., Teri, and all the other women who came to watch me on the field and follow me off of it.

Even so, I never promised Ellie Pleasaunt I'd be faithful. A star has a right to his fun.

MOSTLY, ELLIE SAW TWO or three games each homestand. When I hadn't seen her in the box seats, I thought she was home in Natchitoches with her folks. Sometimes after the game, she drove back the same night, sometimes stayed with her cousin Hattie in Shreveport, sometimes with me. I'd been to Cousin Hattie's with Ellie. She lived at the Knolls Apartments on Jesuit Avenue.

I'd once visited Ellie's folks in Natchitoches, too.

"Come in, Mr. Wyz—," Ellie's ma had said the first time I showed up.

"*Wyzinski*, Mother," Ellie'd said. "He's Polish."

"Praise the Lord, you're as handsome, Mr. Wyzinski, as Ellie said. Pardon me, I was just cleaning up around here. Mr. Pleasaunt will be home soon and we can all sit down to get acquainted. Come right in, son."

Good people, Christians, but love counts for something, too. When we were alone, Ellie'd get over her reservations about sin, and we'd be together in the name of love and ancient Egypt, and she got pregnant.

This particular night, though, I needed time off from all the family stuff to figure how to get out of my slump. It was August. Things weren't so hot at the park. After a few times around the league, I'd stopped seeing the ball. My throws to second were off. Guys stole too easily on me. The skipper really started losing interest in me after my average dropped and my run production dried up because all the love and fame had gone to my head. If the weather didn't wear you down, then thinking of the women of April did. I figured maybe if I just got out on the town like I once did—meet some Louisiana girls, have some drinks—I'd be okay, get my concentration back, then settle in with the one who loved me.

Not ready for sleep, on this hot night I practiced my swing

with the umbrella I'd gotten free at Hall Clothier and Bootery when I was the Prince of Louisiana Avenue. I was killing time in a parking lot swinging at bugs. I hit two moths for homers. "Dodgers' pitcher goes to the mound," I could imagine Vin Scully saying. "Wind blowing in tonight at venerable Candlestick Park. Wyzinski, the batter, steps in."

Around 11:30, with nothing to do, I pulled into a convenience store a thousand miles from the Heartbreak. "How you gals doing?" I said to this lady and her friend running the place. Ready for action, I tried the money clip trick on them.

"Where *you* from?" one of them asked.

"Louisiana."

"You aren't with that funny accent," the other said. Her name was "Honeydew." She was the store clerk. "You got 'America's Dairyland' on your license plates."

"I'm from Louisiconsin, a new state. Superior, Louisiconsin."

"I'm gonna stock the coolers, Joyce hon," Honeydew said, rolling her eyes.

"I'll just get a Yoo-Hoo," I said.

Joyce rang one up the way I now ring up Stashu's vodka or Władziu's blackberry brandy at the Heartbreak.

"My name's Race Gentry," I told her.

Honeydew came out to check on us.

"How you two doing?" she asked.

"He wants to know how old I am. I rang up his Yoo-Hoo."

"You're twenty-seven, aren't you, Joyce?" asked Honeydew.

"Well how about making me an old lady. I swan, I'm not a day over twenty-six."

"I'd a guessed that," I said. "You look great."

Joyce wore these plastic shoes, just strips of white plastic. She had tan legs with little bumps in the skin around the back of her thighs.

"Oh these?" she said when she noticed me looking. "Them's nothing at all. I loofah them away. Look at my hairdo. People tell me I resemble Connie Stevens."

"Who?" I asked.

"The movie star. The actress that once married Eddie Fisher and starred in movies with Troy Donahue."

"Never heard of her," I said.

"Jeez, where you been hiding that you never heard of Eddie Fisher? Jeez, it's a hot night. Lots of stars are out. Why don't we go over to your place and talk a little baseball, honey?"

When we were set to leave, Joyce just opened the front milk cooler and hollered in to her clerk friend, "We're going!"

"Have fun, Joycey. Call me tomorrow," Honeydew yelled from behind the 2%.

I got a Stroh's twelve-pack for the ride. She followed me in her car. I cracked open a beer, turned up the radio, thought of what I'd do to Joyce. Things ain't so bad, I told myself.

She was giggling when she arrived. "I don't much watch sports," she said. "Say, I know where it was! I heard you on radio. You know that Biff Barton guy you see around groshery stores?"

"He's my agent."

"He was on radio advertising Goody's, wa'n't he?"

"Sure, I been on radio with him. Why don't you whisper so we don't wake the neighbors?"

"That's where I heard you," she said.

After drinking two on the way over, I had ten beers left. Joyce carried a few with her. One beer fell from her purse, broke open, fizzed. We were in the third-floor hallway of my apartment building. "I'm destined for the Polish-American Sports Hall of Fame, you know," I whispered, unlocking the door. "What you wearing under that blouse?"

"Oh, hush," she said.

A Yoo-Hoo and three beers later and the blouse was on the floor. It was 1 A.M.; I figured Ellie was home, and Joyce, Honeydew's friend from the convenience store, was dancing to Merle Haggard's "Mama Tried" playing on my stereo. What was I doing? *Crazy with failure. Treadwell called me "Kielbasa"…*

"Sausage Hands." I'd lost my hitting eye. I was trying to get it back with this Joyce lady.

"What's the matter?" she asked when I didn't want to dance right off.

"Nothing. I want to drink. Ain't been feeling so hot lately and I just want a beer. Let's talk about something before we dance."

"Talk! What am I goin' to tell Honeydew? Oh yeah, Honeydew, he was a great guy. We just talked all night. Hon, I'm thirty years old. Well, twenty-nine. I've done enough talking. I want love and romance."

"Lemme just finish my beer."

"No, get up and dance with me. You must know them all. Wa-a- Wa-Watusi."

"You know anything about ancient Egypt?" I said.

"Yeah, that you've got a mummy's curse put on you tonight. I've known guys like you all my life. Flashy big-with-the-talk-guys until you're alone. Then Boris Karloff. Look at me. Jeez, I've been told I'm gorgeous."

When she lowered her head to my shoulder, I felt the stiff hair. It was peroxided blonde, I guess it's called. When she tried to smile seductively, the skin on her face pulled tight. It was like her face couldn't do what her heart wanted.

"Jeez, don't put your hands on my face like you're testing it or something. Jeez, what do you think—I had a facelift? Is that what you're thinking? Jeez, why don't you kiss me?"

Her lips didn't move much when she talked. When I kissed them, she couldn't make them move either. She said her name was Joyce Justine.

"Hush a minute," she said between beers. "I thought I heard something."

"You musta heard a car. Maybe it's my agent's."

"Someone's at the door."

"There's no one at the door," I said. "Let's dance. There's nothing outside either, Joyce. C'mon," I said real fast. "You know how to 'Limbo'?"

"It's the '90s, hon. The limbo went out when I was a teen-ager. I mean I heard it was a '60s dance. I think they play it on Oldies stations sometimes."

"I don't care. Turn up the music. Here, I'll find a song. Go ahead. Limbo. I'll hum it. How l-o-o-o-w can you go-o?"

"No. Listen! You got an 'Augie' here in this building? Is that you?" Joyce asked.

"Augie?" the plaintive voice outside the door said.

"The hell!" Joyce said. "You told me Race. Who's Augie?"

"I'm telling you, my name's Race Gentry. Lemme call my agent to see. There's no one at the door. There's an Augie upstairs, come to think of it. He's a bartender."

When Joyce, half naked, opened the door, I tried to push it shut. The neighbors were standing in bathrobes, angry, mur-muring to each other. They'd been awakened by Ellie beating on doors asking mournfully for Augie.

"Don't disturb me," I said to her as I stepped outside. "Get out of here now like you're supposed to do when I'm busy, Ellie. What you doing here? I had a hard day. Tell all these folks to go back in their apartments."

"I'm pregnant," Queen Nefertiti was saying. She was crying.

"Well I had a damn hard day. I'm trying to relax."

"Race, are you really an all-star?" Joyce was saying, popping her head out from inside the apartment. "Who's this weeping beauty?"

"An all-star with one homer? He's had one round-tripper in two months," said Mr. Youngblood from downstairs.

I thought Ellie was gonna faint.

"*One*," Joyce said. "One home run?"

The other neighbors started in. When he was ogling Joyce, Jack Wright said I was an all-star fool. When I looked back in, Joyce was fixing her blouse, grabbing her purse. "You told me the name Race Gentry meant fifty home runs. Who's this out here callin' for you? Are you *married*?" Joyce hissed.

Poor Ellie, pregnant, looked deathly white when Joyce rushed past.

Drunker than I thought, I tripped on the stairs, could've permanently hurt myself, hurt my throwing arm. "No one was here, Ellie," I was yelling. "I was alone. You're seein' things."

Jeezus, I thought, when I didn't have my car keys. By the time I fished them out of my pocket, both gals were gone. Driving as fast as I could, head spinning, I went by Corky's Townhouse South Restaurant, past Morgan Coffee, Shreve City Gulf. As I looked for Ellie and Joyce, I wondered what a Polack from Yankeeland was doing mixed up with Connie Stevens and Ellie Pleasaunt in Louisiana. Why hadn't I been assigned to Triple-A International League Buffalo, a good Polish town, or Double-A Scranton-Wilkes Barre?

Hung over, out of gas, I had on KEEL-Radio when the sun came up. I waited for Mr. Barton's voice over the airwaves to tell me what to do. If he'd said, "Go to Winn-Dixie, buy a hundred packages of Goody's," I would have. If he'd told me, "Go to Wal-Mart, greet people in my name," I would have done that. I had no one else now, and he knew how to call the Game of Life with 50,000 watts behind him.

When I phoned, Ellie was at Hattie's.

"I'm out on King's Highway," I told Ellie when I got her to come to the phone. "It isn't what you think."

"I don't want to bother with you anymore," she said.

"What can I do all day without you?"

"I can't talk. Hattie's gotta go to work," she said, hanging up.

When I got Joyce on the phone, she hung up, too. She'd telephoned around town. Made a lot of calls about me. Maybe she'd called Fair Grounds Field. "I fooled you anyway, Augie Gentry or whatever your name is," Joyce said. "Because I'm pushing fifty and you didn't notice." She called me "Sausage Glove" and slammed down the phone.

Then it was just me, Augie Wyzinski, listening to the dial tone. I waited and waited for Mr. Biff Barton's voice over the radio, over the phone. Jesus, I needed the sound of him for a minute. Nothing came on the radio, just ads for Pamida, Farmer Brown's Chicken, a few country songs, more ads. Where was talk radio? I went through a tank of gas between 7 A.M. and 1 P.M. driving Louisiana Avenue, I-20, then on the Barksdale Highway to Bossier City. "Do you know Biff Barton?" I asked anyone I saw. "Where can I find Biff, the Voice of the Captains?"

Messed up in the head as I was, I remembered Ellie talking about the gardenias that bloomed in front of her folks' house. On January days, you could smell them through the window, she'd said.

"Mama was hinting you should come back here in winter. Come see us," I remember Ellie saying. "If you don't, I'll send you a gardenia up north." She took my hand then. "You'll have a gardenia in the snow to remind you of me."

I recalled it so well. *What had happened in two months?* Thinking of Ellie and her parents as I sat in a parking lot in the rising August heat broke my heart. They were only seventy miles away. I turned the radio on, listening for Mr. Biff Barton. Where was he, a voice that in summer came out of the very heart of the country where you were … a voice that told you there's this field under a blue sky where an organ can be heard, where people cheer, yell, and grow lonely in the late innings of losing games or toward the end of the season when autumn nears? This same voice tells you a catcher has responsibilities. He backs up first on infield ground balls, blocks wild pitches, explodes from the crouch to gun down the base stealers of the world. But I couldn't do it, couldn't get it done on the field, and now I'd blown it with the only girl who mattered to me.

By two o'clock, it was a hundred degrees out. It looked like rain. On the dirt road that leads to Bayou Clarence, I listened to heat bugs … watched the cattle egrets stepping gently in the water. I was sick. I do not know why a man does such things as

I'd done. Why he cannot be faithful to one who loves him. Is it the price of fame? When you think you're above every citizen of Caddo Parish, Louisiana, because you're on a record home run streak, can you hurt and disregard them all?

"Kielbasa. From now on you're Augie Kielbasa," the skipper'd said a month earlier. "Why don't you wear a sausage to catch with? Wear one on your head while you're at it."

From that night on in Little Rock, Midland, or wherever it was through the whole last half of the Texas League season, I meant nothing to Mr. Treadwell with my .060 batting average and twenty passed balls.

A Christian man, the skipper would always say, "Morals are important and my boys gotta be good men on the diamond and off. Always cherish the temple of the body. Honor that temple. You live right and good off the field, you'll play right and good on the field. That's all we ask. Don't let no weaknesses of the soul and body destroy you in this Game of Life."

I guess he knew why my game had suffered. I'd struggled to get my hitting eye back, but it was like everything I'd done acting so crazy with women and drinking made me lose my edge. I'd forget what signal I just gave. A pitch in the dirt wouldn't get blocked. Thinking about it all made it worse. What about folks waiting for news of me in the *Evening Telegram* back home? How could I let them down?

By now it was 3:30. I was exhausted from the long day, not to mention the crazy night before. I missed Ellie so much. I turned the car around to head to the stadium for tonight's ball game against the Arkansas Travelers. I was done in with regret and shame. I feared for the future. What would come of me?

Since mid-July, when I'd become the bullpen catcher, I heard the skipper Treadwell and Biff Barton talking as I warmed up the pitcher before games. Today when I got to the park, the Voice of the Captains seemed to know I'd been searching the dial for his voice—but he spoke to the skip as if nothing had happened.

"After the weekend, only six games left," Biff was saying.

"We'll probably have El Paso in the playoffs, Biffy," the skipper was saying. Turning to me, he said, "Kid, you're startin'. Les us get a game out of you tonight." Some of his tobacco juice landed on me.

"Looks plum wore out," said Biff Barton. "Keepin' your nose clean, kid?"

Feeling pretty ragged, I didn't say nothing back.

"It's gonna rain," said the skipper. "I cain't risk the new young kid come in last week. The big club when they sent us Farrell last week told us, 'Go easy ... don't hurt Farrell. Get him in his playing time, but don't hurt him. He's a real prospect.' Les us just see what Augie's got or ain't got. Dry off from the drizzle, Kielbasa-Hands. You're startin' tonight. You aren't too tired, are you?"

"I had some trouble with my girlfriend last night."

"Moral trouble?" the skip said. "Baptist trouble?"

"How'd you know?"

"Don't they teach you how to play it straight up north?" he asked. "Thas a problem."

As he stared at me, the rain started. I strapped on shin guards, chest protector, mask ... the so-called "tools of ignorance" because only a fool crouches behind home plate. The Voice of the Captains yelled to me he was going to transmit my name to thousands of fans. He hung out his banner. KEEL-Radio would simulcast in Polish and English, he said, the first-ever Polish-English broadcast of a Texas League game.

Then I heard the crowd, organist, vendors, and heard Mr. Barton start his broadcast with observations on the catcher, 00. And I knew all the members in the National Polish-American Sports Hall of Fame in Orchard Lake, Michigan, were listening, waiting for me to join them. I'd read about them, seen programs Uncle Louie sent from the induction ceremonies: Stan "the Man" Musial in 1973; Ted Kluszewski in '74; in'75, Aloysius Harry Szymanski (Simmons), who was voted MVP with the Philadelphia A's and the next year, 1930, won the batting crown; Stan (Kowaleski) Coveleski in '76 ... on and on, Eddie (Lopatynski) Lopat, Bill Mazeroski, Bill "Moose" Skowron, Tony Kubek ...

5. Hopeful Future Hall of Famer Sees Plans Change

At 8:34 I struck out. It was the sixth inning. KEEL's every watt carried it. When Treadwell came out, the public address system switched to polkas. There was "Pennsylvania Polka," "She's Too Fat Polka," "Liechtensteiner Polka." Fans groaned and started chanting "Ban Polka! Ban Polka!"

"I cain't put in no one else before the playoffs because orders from the big club tell me to keep Farrell benched on rainy nights so he don't hurt his arm or twist his knee," the skipper said through the rain. "So what do I do? You're good for nothin', Kielbasa. Even your music stinks."

As the grounds crew unrolled the tarp in the rain that was falling harder now, Treadwell's face got redder and redder. Someone had told him what had happened with Joyce in my apartment building. He didn't like being embarrassed by his players. Rain dripping from the bill of his cap, he cussed, spit his tobacco. Was Biff analyzing my life moves?

How do you go back to local programming, you wonder in the rain with the last polka playing? Some other night in years to come the skipper will be chewing tobacco, Biff Barton saying, "Good evening, Caps fans," the stadium vendors hawking their goods while cars and trucks on Highway I-20 outside the ballpark whip across America. It's like nothing ever changes down there. *What will Ellie be doing that night, talking to someone else about flowers? As she reads the paper, will her eye catch a story on the Shreveport Captains? Will her ma ask, "Ellie, do you ever think of that nice young man? Your father asks about him from time to time." Will Ellie tell her, "No, Mama, not much anymore ... But look how nice the gardenias are blooming?"* Now there was an empty stadium. The rain they'd predicted all day was forming puddles and streams behind home plate when I saw Ellie walking through the box seats of section C, her pink blouse soaked.

"Why didn't I keep you a secret?" she was asking, wiping rain from her forehead. I knew she was no ghost. She was down on the field. Only two other people were left in the ballpark.

"I shouldn't have taken you to meet my parents this summer." She was running her hands along the screen behind home plate; and I was thinking how, when I'd first gone to Natchitoches with Ellie, her mother and father had said, "Sit down, young man, we saved you a place." It'd all changed by late August. Ellie was saying, "I want to get away from here. I'll apologize at home to my folks, apologize to Hattie—"

The groundskeeper was talking to Mr. Barton. They surprised us. Standing in the shadows, they looked like a part of the ballpark.

"Leave the lights on for them?" the groundskeeper was asking.

"Sure," the Voice of the Captains said.

From under the umbrella the groundskeeper held for him, Biff Barton yelled over, "Kid, you know this might be it for you. If you were famous here and hitting .330, they'd forgive you for fooling around with all those women. But with the way you've gone ... Next year's fans are going to ask, 'Where's the Polish boy? We don't see 00. Where's Kielbasa Kid?' 'He got released,' I'll have to say."

"I know. Tell 'em I'll tend bar up north or sweep floors at the flour mill like my dad does. I can practice my swing in the boiler room for a comeback. I'll get a tryout somewhere."

"You come live down here and straighten out," Mr. Barton was saying. "Stay here, kid. Start a life where you'll pause at the screen door after work ... dream of what might've been if you'd gotten the extra base hit in Tulsa. Then you can go inside, see her fixing your supper and how beautiful she is no matter what she's doing, and be glad you have turned into a hardworking Christian who once had a shot at the big show. There's one decent thing to do, Wyzinski. Why not stay south here, work for the cotton oil plant or for that little college in Natchitoches? Cut grass for the college till you get settled. Maybe when the Caps release you, you can take responsibility—fix car radiators for Ates Radiator or something. We've all made mistakes."

"I wonder if I can, Mr. Barton. Maybe I could get into the insurance business," I said, thinking to myself that "moral prospects" is what the skip and Mr. Barton were wanting us to be—good players with clear consciences who didn't have defects of soul and heart, defects that would hurt them no matter what they did in life.

When I saw beautiful, innocent Ellie still standing in the rain, I believed there was hope if she'd give me a chance to change my life. She was smoothing the wet hair from her face, listening to Biff.

"Then you got a kid steps in like this one they protected, this straight-arrow, non-drinking, non-womanizing prospect Farrell," Biff Barton was saying. "Kid, most folks aren't going anyplace in life but the feed store, the insurance business, the lumber mill day in and day out. They're just ordinary moral folks. It's raining tonight, so they're home. They've got families. Tomorrow they'll go to work, struggle along, pay the bills. Are you going to join us?"

"Sure," I said.

When Mr. Barton held his fingers like an umpire signaling the count, I was thinking how I'd once hit safely in eight straight games. *That* should mean something to God and the Blessed Virgin.

"Three and two. Runner on first is going," Mr. Barton said. "This pitch could decide it." When he said that, he turned on his heel and walked away.

The rain came so hard then I thought Ellie and I'd be washed off the field. She was looking at the frightening sky.

"You shouldn't have come to Natchitoches. You got my folks believing in us," she said.

"Tell them I didn't want it to turn out wrong."

"It don't matter now," she said.

When she told me she never loved me—not even at the start—her voice breaking, I knew I'd had my chance, that she'd given me her heart and I'd broken it and that she would go away. I'd turn into an immoral gaboosh who'd work in places like the Heartbreak, recalling the might-have-beens Biff Barton had told me about.

"Too much is wrong with you," she was saying, crying. I didn't hear what else she said as she opened the gate by the dugout where the sign on the fence says No Pepper Games.

When the Voice of the Captains and the groundskeeper escorted her through the dark runway beneath the stands, nobody asking whether I could do better, nobody giving me a second chance, I realized what remained was for them to shut off the lights on my chances for happiness with Ellie and on my one chance at making the Polish-American Sports Hall of Fame.

I sat all night in the dark stadium, regretting what would become of me. Lots of people hurt and betray others. She didn't deserve it. I should've valued her the way I valued making the Hall of Fame. I didn't think or know much last season. But it hits me now that these memories are the tools of ignorance I am left with, so I put them on and regret who I am.

6. Ex-Minor Leaguer Joins County Beer League

A season later, I wipe the bar at the Heartbreak Hotel and turn the radio dial when the jukebox is off. Over the airwaves of the South last year, signals were crisscrossing, bringing me together with folks like Mr. and Mrs. Pleasaunt, like Ellie, like Biff… good, ordinary folks. Folks who lived plain, quiet lives. A life in Louisiana would've been good for me, too: Captains' broadcasts, the summer skies Biff Barton talked about, Ellie on walks by Cane River, reminding me of my hitting streaks and pulling out newspaper clippings she'd once saved about me. There'd be faithful church attendance and a baby to love and rear. *Oh, Ellie, I've learned what I never knew last season: You were trusting and honest and I let you down. I looked for a flower, a gardenia, this January, but you didn't send one.*

Nowadays till someone at the end of the bar—till Pete, say—needs the services of a washed-up ballplayer (of a gaboosh like him), I imagine a voice a long way off in the rain. I can hear you, Ellie, walking away with that voice from the radio I knew so well.

Nowadays, circling the bases in the Old Timers' League up here in Douglas County, wearing this wool uniform in Sunday's heat, I think of you. For each rocket I hit, the owner of Heartbreak buys me a Fitger's beer and a package of string cheese. My signing bonus was a job here and Sundays off to hit homers for you and me, the catcher and you, Ellie—who will never be together after last year's season of lies. I hit home runs of a kind never seen before. You can believe this. Home runs that tear out my heart, home runs that are talked about in this league of nobodies.

"Augie?"

"Yeah, Pete?" I say.

"What ya thinkin' about?"

"Nothing," I say. "A girl."

"Who?"

"I'll tell you later, but now I'm gonna think about runners I threw out in Jackson, of the great two-hit game I called for Bill Chambliss in Midland-Odessa. A catcher has responsibilities, you know, Pete."

I shake his hand as he slumps against the wall. I shake all their hands. My East End fans. The Hamm's clock ticks on, the sign sizzles. The gabooshes shuffle to the jukebox, the men's room, the pachinko game to try to roll a nickel down the right path. Things never change at Heartbreak Hotel.

"Thanks," I say to them, to ham-faced Władziu, to Stashu, to Benny.

"*Dziękuję*," they say. "You had a goot career in baseball."

"Thank you, Paul," I say.

"Yeah, Augie."

"Thank you, too, Casimir."

"You bet, Augie. Glad you're home."

"Thank you, John."

"Tank *you*, Augie. Strike three for you?"

"Here's a toast to all you guys for telling me how bad I was at the game," I say. "Next we're getting the neon sign fixed. I'll talk to the boss. We aren't heartbroke, so why should we have a broken sign? Well, maybe Pete is. Pete, you're pickled. Why don't you go home? Can you walk, or should I call you a cab?"

"*You* go home!"

"I can't. What would I do? Sit with my ma? Say the rosary with her? Anyway, if I looked in the mirror at home, I'd just see you guys. I might as well stay here where I got you in front of me. Go on, tell me I'm lousy. I got all night to listen to you guys with high self-esteem."

Time Between Trains

Five days a week, the track inspector checked the rail line from the Superior, Wisconsin, waterfront up to Chub Lake, Minnesota. From the cab of his rail truck, he reported undercuts and washouts to the radio dispatcher at the rail yard in Superior. During dry spells, he looked for fires set by train sparks.

With a track warrant for every portion of his journey, he went along in the special truck with its rubber tires for road and highway travel and flanged, locomotive-style wheels for railroad travel. To switch from one to the other mode, he'd center the truck at a crossing, climb down, grab a metal pole to insert into the wheel mechanism, and raise the steel, flanged wheels, leaving the rubber tires resting on the track. Backing up the truck, he'd stop, turn the steering wheel, drive forward, and be back on dirt or pavement.

In his fourteen years with the Burlington Northern Santa Fe, Joe Rubin looked for sun kinks, broken rails, broken bonds, wood ties left on the tracks, and other potentially deadly defects or impediments on or alongside the way to Chub Lake. When he reported a sun kink (when the sun expands a steel rail, bending it out of place), the section crew got after it. When he reported a pull apart (in bitter cold, railroad tracks contract and pull apart), the section crew came to lay kerosene-soaked ropes next to the rails and waited for the heated track sections to snap together.

Along the east-west tracks before the Crawford Creek signals (where flashing yellow means a track inspector can move onto the main line at Saunders) were the broken ties he reported one day last November. West of there was a section of track ballast to keep an eye on near that boggy run before the Vet's Crossing. Farther along, past Boylston, almost to the signal lights at Milepost 15.9 where the tracks converge, was the hair-thin rail fracture in the right rail of eastbound track he reported last December. How important this work! Thank God for the track inspector.

Naturally, his job required keen senses. In a noisy diesel locomotive pulling twenty-two thousand tons of taconite from the Hibbing, Minnesota, plant down past Kelly Lake terminal to the Superior dock, sometimes a railroad engineer will sense discrepancies in the track. But Joe Rubin was supposed to be first to identify when a track sounded off. He was regional Employee of the Month twice in fourteen years. The award meant much to him, for unlike many employees, he lived for the railroad. Mornings, he cleaned his BNSF hardhat of grease or dirt, whispering absent-mindedly to himself about a section of track he had to examine. Friday evenings, in the kitchen of his apartment by the rail yard, he reviewed his week's performance. The work week over, he was likely to talk aloud to his parents' pictures on the walls of his rooms. On the second and fourth Wednesdays of the month, he got a haircut. All of these were solitary activities, for he wasn't one to say much to a barber.

His week, his life, was made solitary in other ways. He'd had very few girlfriends, which meant no one to telephone about meeting for a drink or going to dinner. He was probably the only Jewish track inspector in a vast BNSF railroad network stretching from here to Fort Worth, and he drove the truck eight hours a day through such long stretches of uninhabited country that he might as well have been in Siberia. BNSF section hands called him "the Wandering Jew." Wanderer or not, this was lonely work. The tracks ran through miles of speckled alder rising black against the snow—through aspen and pine forests, past tamarack bogs and cutover hayfields, out over trestles where you saw frozen rivers meander below. Here and there appeared farmhouses and railroad crossings, but once he had his track warrant on a winter morning and was passing under Tower Avenue westbound on Number 1 main track, he pretty much said good-bye to everyone but the dispatcher. When he was stopped at a crossing or off on a siding while a 170-car taconite train came highballing down Saunders' Grade on the mainline, he'd wave to the engineer; but there was no talking, no laughing with a fellow employee, just Joe Rubin in freshly pressed work clothes standing on the shaking earth or sitting alone in his truck as the brown rail cars thundered past, trailing steam from taconite so hot from the mill that, even parked in the yards, the yet-unloaded ore steamed for three days.

With the last cars flown by, blinking safety light gone out of sight around a curve, quiet returned to the track inspector. Chickadees sang in the aspen trees. Crows circled above. A flock of snow buntings in a quiet cloud rose out of the stark gray branches of a mountain ash. After the train's passing, which disturbed the wildlife more than it did Joe Rubin, he called the dispatcher. "What you got going west? Number ninety-two BNSF is by me now. Can I get a warrant to Chub Lake?" To which the dispatcher might reply, "I've got a taconite train coming out of Allouez dock. I'll be holding a coal train at Chub Lake. You got an hour. Get coffee if you have a place nearby." More often than one might imagine, track inspectors have time between trains.

Though from certain mileposts, Joe Rubin could have raised the flanged wheels and made it to a country café and back, he generally brought a thermos of coffee and a sack lunch to eat. With his windows rolled down, what things he saw on mild winter days as he waited dreamily for the through freight; a spider made its way over the snow by his front tire; an ermine popped its head from the white earth; a snowy owl perched atop a paper birch, looking at the curious world. The delicate, beautiful bird and animal tracks he saw after a fresh snow reminded him of his own work on the tracks. Once Joe Rubin drove his truck into the silent void after a train passed, it was as if the train had never been there—no shrill whistle frightening deer, no diesel smoke—just the smooth gliding of the track inspector on his way to Chub Lake.

EARLY ONE YEAR, HE decided he'd become too passionate about his job, too committed. Through his heavy boots, his legs, even up into his heart, he sensed the slightest problem with railroad tracks. Nothing was too fine to escape the inspector's attention. He took good care of the truck; he worked late; he reported problems before they occurred. He wanted so much to be Employee of the Month again that week after long week he thought of nothing else.

After work on Fridays, he'd stop in a place where for an hour he could be less vigilant of the railroad. Seeing Joe Rubin, someone would yell to Ogy, the bartender, as he rang up a cash register sale, "Play that Jewish piano, Ogy. Make the Jewish piano sing." The track inspector laughed as was expected of him, for he wanted to get along with people. But what some wiseguy yelled to the bartender coupled with "the Wandering Jew" nickname and other small slights made him feel that he might just as well go back out to inspect the tracks. Listening to the sound of rails wasn't so bad, he told himself. He might as well spend the weekend in his truck on a siding, maybe at Milepost 8 or M.P. 12.

AT M.P. 15.9 LIVED A WOMAN who wished she were less solitary. Alone most evenings, Sofia had done well in life, at least for Superior. She was a teacher in an elementary school outside town, eight miles east of her home. "Mrs. Stepan," the children called her, though she was a widow, and her married name now had a sad, hollow ring in her ears.

She lived at the four corners where South Irondale Road crosses County Trunk Highway C, then winds through thick woods down into a river valley.

Sofia's house was the only building at the corners. Across the highway and the BNSF tracks were the wooden M.P. 15.9 sign and the gray railroad masts that told east- and westbound trains to hold or proceed. In midsummer when everything greens up, the area is unremarkable, unnoticeable. In other corners of the intersection were ditches dug out of the clay, a few scraggly alder and hawthorn bushes, and miles of fields that ended in the woods where, forty years ago, her father hunted rabbits. Twenty times a day trains passed—every five minutes a truck or automobile on the paved highway came close to the house, but nothing slowed, nothing stopped except once in a while a train on Number 1 track being held until the eastbound line was clear. Otherwise nothing, no reason to stop, though sometimes a truck driver speeding by might wave if he spotted Sofia staring out her bedroom window on the highway side of the house. At least there was something to see that way. Her other windows looked out on empty fields.

Five days a week during the school year she was busy, and then, in June and July, there was summer school. Sofia loved her third-graders; but after teaching them and reading to them, correcting arithmetic and penmanship, escorting them to the playground, coordinating milk breaks, meeting parents, taking care of the small and large responsibilities of a teacher's day, she found the job growing more tedious each year. For twenty-five years she'd done the work. During the January that Joe Rubin fully realized the extent of his commitment to his job, concentrating on railroad tracks to the exclusion of everything else, Sofia stared from her bedroom window and wondered where the years had flown. Her husband, Jerry Stepan, had been dead ten years, she had two women-teacher friends she saw socially once a month, and she lived alone in her house with shiplap siding at a boring crossroads in a flat country above a river valley. With a class of eight-year-olds clamoring for her attention, Sofia had less time than the track inspector for introspection. Still, as much of her time as they took and as much as she delighted in the children, she knew her life was passing.

As she daydreamed out at the fields, sometimes her life seemed empty, but then she would snap herself out of her reverie and return to her pupils' work or listen to records as she reheated coffee in a pan on the stove. Maybe everyone feels this way in winter, she thought. Sofia had a few moments in the evenings to think like this, or on weekends after finishing the dishes and preparing her school clothes; but the track inspector, during every long season, had plenty of time to worry over where his life was going.

Though neither knew it, they traveled parallel tracks. The highway runs beside the tracks (except for the ditch between) until "Shortcut Road," where Sofia turned down a dirt road to pick up South State Highway 35 to school. Four or five times a year as he was heading to Chub Lake and she was on the way to or from Nemadji Elementary, they rode close to each other, the proximity occurring more often when he had time between trains—for the tracks at M.P. 15.9 are only a few steps farther from the house than from the highway. To Joe Rubin what did it matter that sometimes there was a woman driving parallel to him at the same speed he was going? Since the old neighborhood of Jews on Connors' Point had vanished, he thought there was no one worth noticing. His people had intermarried or moved away—everyone but the track inspector, who'd put off marriage to care for his parents. When his father died, the synagogue closed; the remaining old people went to Adas Israel in Duluth. Right before his mother died, the boarded-up Hebrew Brotherhood Synagogue in Superior (where his parents once had to reserve seats during High Holidays because of the large turnout of people) was set on fire. Over and over in the last weeks of her life, his mother said to Joe, "This isn't how it should end." As if to support her claim, her burial left the Hebrew Cemetery filled to capacity.

Busy as he was, Joe Rubin didn't often go to visit his parents' graves, and there was nothing left to see of the synagogue.

He concerned himself with a different kind of particulars now. He'd become a detective, you might say. At work, he carried with him a small book. In some dreary northern place, when he got out of the truck to stretch, he compared pictures of animal tracks in the book to tracks he saw in ditches and fields, or sometimes running along or between the railroad tracks. Sometimes these mammal tracks made exquisite designs. Magnified, the smallest of them—shrew tracks—looked like hands with long, crooked fingers growing sharp and thin at the end. He learned that "long-tailed shrews frequently leave a tail mark on their trail, which is barely over an inch-wide." During the course of his investigation, he read in *Mammals of the Superior National Forest* that "red fox prints appear as a line of prints as if the animal were walking along a string. A fox track is roughly circular and 1.5-2 inches in diameter. In soft snow where detail cannot be seen, their tracks appear as a line of round depressions."

Sometimes he confused mammal tracks with the tracks made by birds' claws. The way they went out over the fields, on out into the distance, all these (if you pretended) could be the tracks of people like the wandering inspector. The variety of mice living in the area presented problems in track identification, too. Above the snow and tunneling beneath it, they left an artistic network Joe Rubin got on his knees to observe. What was so unusual about his kneeling in snow? Joe wondered. Old-time railroad workers broke out a pint of brandy or a couple of miniatures of whiskey or vodka to keep *them* company. At least what Joe Rubin did endangered no one. Kneeling in his brown jacket and insulated pants, he looked as if he were praying as he searched for the animal tracks, which, to him, seemed to represent the Diaspora of the Jews.

As he was doing this searching that resembled praying one afternoon while the schools celebrated Martin Luther King Jr.'s birthday and when he himself waited for a taconite train to pass, a voice startled him. The track bed, the tracks, the gray signal masts looked especially forlorn. All morning, a biting wind ducked low over the fields. Now this voice—"You grow to be like the company you keep."

Turning, he saw a woman in the middle of Number 2 track.

She said it again in what he thought must be Polish, "You become like the company you keep ... *Z kim przestajesz takim sié stajesz.*"

She walked down the slight pitch in the road, crossed the highway, and went into her house, wondering, the teacher, why she hadn't walked toward the river on her day off. She sat a half-hour in her coat and gloves pondering it.

Now that he had seen her, she wouldn't catch him so deep in thought again.

When he heard her call to the rural mail carrier one afternoon, "Yes, it's a nice day," several months had passed. He'd traveled hundreds of miles round-trip from Superior to Chub Lake. He'd seen the spring sun erase mouse and hare tracks in the snow. He'd even noticed willows along the route turning yellow. Their leaves would appear in a month.

Two nights in February, on the other hand, she'd stayed at school for open house. One night in March, she had drunk too much Irish coffee, finding herself staring at the M.P. 15.9 sign. Another night that month, she had reread all her husband's letters, whispering "Jerzy" in Polish.

In April, when the wind is sharp (wind that sounds like her husband's name), then in the shelter of ditches bloom delicate cowslips, which her husband had called marsh marigolds. He'd ask in letters from Buffalo, New York, or Lorain, Ohio, "Are the marsh marigolds blooming, Sofia?"

"The cowslips, don't you mean?" she'd answer, jokingly.

He never bothered to correct her. A wheelsman on the ore boat *William F. Sutter*, he drowned in a Lake Michigan storm when the marsh marigolds were blooming back home. As a widow she learned that the chaliced, yellow flowers with heart-shaped leaves really are called marsh marigolds as often as cowslips. Each year for the ten years since her husband's death, they bloomed. Each April she was sad.

She didn't know the track inspector's name, but on her way to school, she was aware of his truck on the tracks paralleling the highway. She knew from a lifetime of learning important and unimportant facts that James. J. Hill, the Empire Builder, had brought the railroad through here in the late 1800s, that her dear mother came from a part of Poland now called Silesia, that Douglas County has high unemployment, that a *bulbul* is a Persian bird, that the moisture content of hay in silos has to be checked to be sure that the hay doesn't combust, that cowslips are marsh marigolds, and that during the Middle Ages, Poland was a haven for Jews. She knew this last like she knew what a trapezoid is—or a parallelogram (her husband had accumulated compasses, rulers, protractors). What she knew about Catholic Poland and the Jews, that miscellaneous fact, would matter to Joe Rubin and the teacher. Now in a gusty April, however, she sat in the place where roads cross, the lonely four corners where, with nothing stopping it, the wind sweeps along without regard for anything.

When she was thinking of the track inspector—which she did at odd moments, happy to know that if he was at M.P. 15.9 then her house would be safe from intruders—the wanderer was thinking of her. When he had time, he'd surprise her, stand at the crossroads, wave to her. What did she mean saying he would become like the company he kept when he had no company? He imagined he saw those who really mattered, the people of the Diaspora, in the winter prints and tracks, in the forest shadows when the snow left, in the brown grass of fields, in the pictures on his walls. He could trace them back to Noah. His ancestors had remained four hundred and thirty years in Egypt. Such was the company Joe Rubin kept! If he hadn't found a home and still wandered the earth, enduring hardship and insult, such was his lot, he told himself as he radioed the dispatcher for a track warrant.

The one thing Sofia Stepan did with delight was to grow a garden out of sight of the railroad tracks and the county trunk highway. Except for this garden, she in no other way indulged herself. Though the garden stood in sunlight all afternoon on the south side of the house, by six o'clock—no matter the warmth of the day—it was cool and quiet. There she grew aster, yarrow, phlox, black-eyed Susan, hollyhock, butterfly bush. Coreopsis and lantana were not unknown to her. From flower to flower fluttered cabbage butterflies, mourning cloaks, monarchs, swallowtails. One afternoon she counted sixty-five butterflies. Sofia thought the butterflies could impart something of their beautiful delicacy to you in proportion to how much peace and strength you needed after a decade of disappointments.

Though Joe Rubin hadn't seen her garden, he often thought of the woman at the crossroads. In May, convinced that the language she spoke was Polish and that she appeared to like seeing him at Milepost 15.9, he thought of no one else but her. One evening in the Hebrew Cemetery, where he hadn't been in months, he wondered exactly what kind of company she kept, this Polish woman. The names on the gravestones echoed his question—Lurye, Sher, Vogel, Pomush, Edelstein, Kaner, Cohen, Marcovich, Handlovsky ... The old people knew Polish. They'd lived in Poland. "You become like the company you keep."

As is customary, atop his parents' graves he placed a few stones from the cemetery road. They symbolized a rock-strewn desert landscape and how all are equal in death. He gathered a few stones to keep in his pocket. He prayed for his parents' souls, spoke aloud to them as the warm, spring breeze swept through the willow groves along the river below the cemetery. Stones on a grave are more permanent than flowers.

On the way home, he decided the next time the Polish woman was at work he would cross the highway and walk down Irondale Road past her house. What was the harm in going by her place? Polish Jews and Polish gentiles had lived together for centuries.

Before he had a chance to do so, it was June. Her garden had been transformed by gentle rains, by the warm sun on the side of the house no one saw. As the third week of summer school passed, there were more butterflies in Sofia's garden than she'd ever seen. The flowers and bushes she planted attracted them. She wanted to read her husband's letters aloud to them all day long; but in addition to a morning filled with teaching, she'd agreed to perform certain administrative tasks in the afternoon. When she finished, she hurried home.

She was still at school when Joe Rubin saw the company she kept. Even from the road, he couldn't believe his eyes. Flying about, carried on slight, warm breezes, the butterflies in Sofia's garden looked like colorful patches of silk. They tumbled and fluttered, purple, yellow, orange, blue, lighting on the flowers, glancing against the bright, delighted leaves. No one but the Wandering Jew saw them, in his pocket the stones from the cemetery, which in his amazement at what he was seeing, he'd left on the road in front of her house and in her yard.

When Sofia returned home at four o'clock, she thought at first it was Jerzy in the butterfly garden. "Jerzy?" she cried, thinking her theory was right about the peace and strength butterflies bring to those in need. She thought perhaps her husband had brought her a letter and hadn't drowned at all. How everything was going to be good again, she whispered to herself. This was especially true on so colorful an afternoon. The hills were brilliant, the fields, the yard, the butterfly garden. She thought how she'd love Jerzy more than a person could possibly love anyone.

When she saw who it really was, however, and that this was no sailor's ghost of Jerzy Stepan with a love letter, her heart fell. It took her a moment, several moments, to consider what she faced on such a lovely afternoon with work over and the house empty. After a lifetime of loving someone, it's not easy to change. But then she murmured very softly, "That's all right. You can come in," to the lonely man who all winter had looked for mouse, hare, and fox tracks and who now gently swept the butterflies from his shirt and hands before he went through the door into her life.

A Chance for Snow

My brother's name is Steven. We're playing outdoors. The earth is frozen. "Leave me alone," I tell him when he teases me.

"Agnes! You and Stevie come in!" Mother calls. "Agnes, do you hear?"

Beyond the fields, steam rises over the largest freshwater lake in the world. Above the wind, we hear the waves crash in.

"Look at the clouds out there," Steven says.

"It's like that when the water's warmer than the air," I tell him. "Being in grade school has taught you nothing. You're stupid."

Sometimes he bugs me so much that I call him by our last name, Stasiak, pronounced "Stashok." "There's a fungus among us. Get out of here," I warn him when he wants to talk to me and I'm with my girlfriends. When I do this, it's like Stevie's a member of another family.

"Why is it so dark over the lake?" he asks.

"I told you. It's the cloudy sky and the sea smoke."

He draws a stick man on the frost at the bottom of the window.

"Get out of the cold," Dad says from the kitchen.

"Close the door after you," I tell my brother.

Dad asks, "Did you rake the leaves?"

"Yes. Is Cliff coming over?" I ask. Cliff is his pal from work. They practice their music on Wednesdays. Sitting at the kitchen table, Cliff playing the banjo, Dad the accordion, they play "Julida Polka," "Blue Skirt Waltz," and "Under the Double Eagle." They practice all the time but never play anywhere.

At the table, Stevie mimics me when no one's looking. Then we eat supper.

"It's Wednesday. That means Cliff," Dad says afterward as if reminding himself. In the next room, he opens the accordion case. He carries the accordion into the kitchen. Sticking his arms through the straps, he undoes the fastener holding the bellows. He never closes the door between rooms, thinking we like hearing him play "The Pennsylvania Polka" over and over in the kitchen.

Stevie crawls under the table. Dad will play a song then quit for a moment. If he goofs, he starts again. Now he plays "American Patrol."

"Don't throw away any of the newspaper when you're done," Dad says to us as he plays some more. Among the paper's headlines "Harvest dinner Sunday … Local Elks host state rep," he has circled the Soo Passages, which lists the boats heading through the locks at Sault Ste. Marie. Upbound for Superior, Duluth, or Taconite Harbor are the *Roger M. Keyes, Ralph Misener, Sparrows Point, Cartercliffe Hall*, and a Polish ship, the *Ziemia Opolska*.

It is confining in the small space under the table where Stevie's gone. There's the risk of Dad's foot stepping on him. Stevie waits for Dad to arrange his sheet music. He kind of tickles the side of Dad's shoe, runs his fingers along the toe, which he polishes with his shirt cuff. "Thank you, Steven," Dad says. When the music begins, so does the foot—up, down, up, down, tapping out "Helena Polka." Stevie times the foot. He slips his hand in and out of danger beneath Dad's shoe. "Ouch!" my brother cries. His head flies up. It bangs the bottom of the table. "We'll put him in the warmest room upstairs," Dad says, holding Stevie's hand down with his shoe. "Ow, Ouch," Stevie cries, though his hand's not really hurt.

"Sorry," Dad says.

"Who we putting where?" I ask as Stevie shakes his fingers and rubs his head.

"Your dad's got something on his mind," Mother says.

Stevie heads upstairs when he hears the doorbell. "I'm itchin' to try a new arrangement," Cliff says. He tunes and strums his banjo. I'm angry about the racket and lose track of my stupid brother. Even upstairs you can hear "Lady of Spain." The ceiling blocks the music a little, but it still comes up muffled through the vent. If I shut the vent when I'm up there, Dad will think I don't like his music. He thinks we're fortunate having a guest artist like Cliff Christensen over every week.

When I look for Stevie, he's already asleep, and it's still early. As long as I can remember, I've been listening to kitchen band concerts. I've had so much experience that I can identify "Beautiful Ohio," "When Your Old Wedding Ring Was New," and "Hoop Dee Doo Polka" by how fast or slow the musicians tap their feet.

In three upstairs rooms, Dad has placed Holy Water and Holy Candles. In mine, a small crucifix hangs from the window frame, and I have a larger cross over the bed. From each side of my vanity, I've hung rosaries, and the vanity's six small drawers are filled with prayer books. In the front of one of them is a calendar of the "Great Days of My Youth." Dad has written in it how Agnes Elizabeth Stasiak made her First Holy Communion on May 19, 1983.

Now we're up to St. Elizabeth of Hungary in the liturgical year. I lie in bed wondering what my patron saint was like, what the old country was like. I think about a lot of things as Dad and Cliff play like they have a big concert or something coming up at the Duluth Arena.

Our visitor comes the next day when me and Stevie are in school. "I threw my arms around him. I welcomed him," Dad says.

In the kitchen, the visitor smiles at us. "We only met once," Dad says about him. "I gave him our name and our address that time. 'Write to us,' I told him. But who'd think he'd turn up here? I was kidding yesterday about putting him upstairs. Every time a Polish boat's in port, the sailors go to the Kosciuszko Club." Dad says a couple of words in Polish.

Here me and Stevie go to school and everything's normal. We study geography, sing, draw, and work arithmetic; we pray the Angelus at 11:30, then we walk home for lunch to find a foreign sailor at our table.

Dad says, "This is my son."

"Stefan?" the sailor says.

"And Agnes."

"Agnieszka."

When the visitor smiles, his face looks like it's carved from stone. His hair, eyebrows, and eyes are dark brown and stand out against his light skin. There is the small, smiling mouth, and the point of his chin. I don't know what in his face makes him look foreign, but his face is different. He buttons his dark plaid shirt to the collar. "You have nice children," he says, which Dad translates for us.

"They're good kids, too. And where are yours?"

When he answers, Dad says our visitor has no close family left, just friends in Chicago.

"We're his friends, too," Ma says.

"We're your friends," Dad says.

"Yes," says the visitor. He smiles throughout lunch.

"Steven, yours is the warmest room," Dad says.

My brother is as surprised by the visitor as Dad is. For once, my brother keeps quiet during lunch.

Łukasz has come here on the *Ziemia Opolska*, which has sailed from the Atlantic Ocean through the St. Lawrence Seaway then inland to Superior. From the docks on lower Tower Avenue, he's found his way to our house. "He must've practiced how he was going to do all this. How do you beat that?" Dad asks us.

In school that afternoon, nobody knows about him and nothing exceptional has ever happened to my classmates in their lives, which means they're the same as they were an hour ago. But my brother and me are different.

The Sisters at our school are Polish. Many families in the neighborhood are, but these days, they are more American. During afternoon recess, I stare at the pictures of school classes. The class photos hang in the hallway. Some are from 1920 or 1930. A lot of the students in the photographs have come from Poland. There is Dad's class, too.

When Stevie and I get home from school, Łukasz Cedzynski is in Stevie's room. He's brought a duffel bag with clothes. Stevie sits in a chair, looking at him. From the window, we see the Great Sweetwater Sea. The trees down by it have lost their leaves. Everything is gray in November.

"Mr. Cedzynski?" I say.

"No *Angielski*," he replies, smiling. He throws up his hands.

"He don't understand," says Stevie. "C'mon, Mr. Cedzynski," he says, taking the sailor's arm.

Łukasz puts on his shoes to come downstairs with us. When my brother tries getting him outside, the sailor won't go. He just wants to watch the windows steam up.

"Do you want a better coat? Is that what it is?" Stevie says.

"Steven, leave him alone," Mother says. She's baking a ham and potatoes. Dad has driven to a tavern to get something for them to drink.

We make the evening paper. Mr. Cedzynski and Dad are at the table with Stevie setting our places for supper when I bring in the news. The story is on the bottom right-hand corner of page 1: "A sailor was reported missing Thursday from a ship docked at Harvest States Elevator, according to a spokesman for the shipping agency Guthrie-Hubner. The man, a crew member of the *Ziemia Opolska*, may be seeking asylum. An agent in charge of the immigration service's Border Patrol called the incident a 'very sensitive matter.' The *Ziemia Opolska* was scheduled to leave Friday night."

"Keep all this to yourselves," Dad says. As he pours their drinks, Dad reads how asylum seekers must be interviewed by immigration officials, how an application for asylum is then sent to the U.S. State Department, which returns an opinion to the district office in St. Paul on whether "to grant the applicant asylum for a period of one year, pending further review."

As our visitor stares at the newspaper photo of the ship he left, I come to think I've seen his face in pictures in the school hallway. I've seen the same rough hands hanging from sleeves of the students; all the boys in their suits lined up and Father Nowak in the middle. My dad learned English when he got to the U.S. Me and Stevie know only English. I figure some of the students must have missed their birthplace. My grandfathers and all my uncles belong to the Polish Club. Stevie will join when he grows up. Dad has the form ready for him. Also, people still sing Polish carols on Christmas Eve at our church, so that proves they miss the old country. Things have changed over the years, though.

Dad has these government bonds from the old days. The green and white paper has all kinds of scrolls and signatures on them plus an eagle, the symbol of Poland. The National City Bank of New York will pay their value if you cash them in. The paper they are on curls up at the edges. REPUBLIC OF POLAND, it says on them. BOND ISSUE OF 1920. DUE 1ST April 1949. Dad says a good Pole wouldn't accept the money. It'd be like collecting an IOU from a friend or from someone you loved.

Łukasz likes my mother's cooking. He eats well at sea, but not like this, he says to Dad. He tells us inflation is high in Poland, gas rationed, and that you have to stand in line for bread.

"I will be happy to buy as much as I wish here," Łukasz says for Dad to translate. "I will not miss the sea."

"We have our own sea, Lake Superior," Dad says.

After supper, as Stevie and me do the dishes, the sailor gives us a dollar.

When the Duluth paper comes the next morning, there's another story about the defector. "'Immigration office mum on ship jumper,'" Dad reads as Stevie eats breakfast. Mr. Cedzynski is shaving in the bathroom, humming a tune. Listening to Dad, I learn that INS officials will be coming when we're in school and our guest is here in the house. I wish I could see how they look.

"The paper says you're in the area, Mr. Cedzynski," Dad says. "'The sailor has asked Immigration and Naturalization for asylum.' Did you know that, Łukasz? You're famous."

When Dad reads the next part, "Odds appear to be against it," he puts down his coffee. "Seventy-five percent of the Polish Nationals who sought asylum in this country were denied that status last year," he says. "'The sailor must show he is fleeing persecution based on race, religion or political affiliation,' said George Wenzel of the Immigration Service. 'The burden of proof is on the person seeking asylum.'"

I read the rest. At the bottom is a chart with the number of people from different countries that've applied for asylum. In the past five years, from 1983 to 1988, 8,993 Poles have applied in order to escape martial law. There's another picture of the *Ziemia Opolska* in the *Tribune*.

"Good morning," says Łukasz when my brother comes in. Stevie says in Polish, "Good morning."

"It is a nice morning," our visitor says.

"We heard you praying last night," Dad says to me. I pray all through the week.

The next Wednesday Cliff rings the doorbell.

"Say hello to our houseguest," Dad says.

Cliff is surprised to find someone new here. Stevie sits beside Mr. Cedzysnki. When Cliff and Dad start "Helena Polka," my brother ducks under the table. When I look at our visitor, I'm glad Mr. Cedzynski hears me praying for him. He's trying to fit in. To look more natural, he unbuttons his top shirt button.

Though it takes a week, we get him outdoors. After his statement to the officials about why he's left ship, he still doesn't feel safe. He wears Dad's coat. I buy him a stocking cap. Sometime now there is a chance for snow.

We hike the ravine. The creek has frozen. We walk along the Burlington Northern tracks, following the tracks across the river to the Allouez neighborhood where Cliff lives. If you turn south and go out, you'll come to a big trestle that crosses the river again, but upstream from where we are. The trestle runs a half-mile over this swamp. We are up there when Łukasz begins talking. He starts in like he's doing it to hear himself. Going along the walkway are me, Stevie, and Mr. Cedzynski, who does all the talking, saying, "Please, I hope you will help me, God."

Me and my girlfriends always stop halfway across. Sometimes we see an old woman, Mrs. Burbul, under the trestle staring at the river. The trestle is high. In one direction, you see the white birch and the pine trees and beyond, far away in the distance, the Murphy Oil Refinery with the flames burning what are called "off-gasses." In another direction is the highway leaving town, the small bridge we crossed earlier, the lake, and more trees and forests. My brother is very cold. I feel sorry for him and Łukasz. With the wind blowing right through all of us, I ask our visitor what's wrong.

His eyes are so deep and serious that I believe I see the forest in them.

"Mr. Cedzynski," I say.

I think he wants to tell me right then. He tries. But when

he starts, the forest goes out of his eyes. I see his tears. He's talking to himself.

Farther on, we see these delicate spider strands I've noticed before. They're white and very thin, like spider-web material, but only individual threads that aren't forming anything. They float along until they catch on something like a guardrail on a trestle. Sometimes in summer you could run up there and these silver spider threads wrapped around you and for a moment made you rich with silver. When you pull them off a blouse or shirt, they are so light they ride out of sight on the wind. I'm surprised to see the strands so late in the fall.

Dad told me a week before that it isn't hard for Poles to come to this country if they have family already here. It is just difficult for those with no one. They have to seek asylum. They can't get visas. A part of one of the spider threads sticks to Mr. Cedzynski's coat after the walk. It is hanging on the kitchen chair. Mr. Cedzynski's face is red from the cold wind we faced on the trestle. By failing to understand him when he was speaking earlier, I've let him down, I think to myself.

Dad and him talk Polish. Łukasz describes things with his hands, sweeping his arms to show something Stevie and I did. "*Czykago*," he says a couple times.

"He's leaving," Dad says.

I stutter something when Mr. Cedzynski goes upstairs.

"He'll be back, though," Dad says.

"How will he get back?" I ask him.

"Hop a bus, I suppose. It's a nine-hour ride, but so what?"

They are driving up to get him. I've heard them speak of his friends from Chicago who've telephoned a few times. They've gotten letters from Mr. Cedzynski over the past year. "His friends left early to get here by noon," Dad says. "They'll be coming."

They hug Łukasz the way Dad first did. They shake our hands. The Polish lady has already lived in America, but Michał and his wife have only come over and speak no English. Mother serves them cake and rolls. Stevie and me listen. Once in a while, Michał or his wife will say, "How old is your daughter?" or "The children grow up fast." I am part of the language they speak. When they're talking together and Ma's rushing around the house, I don't think I'll miss Łukasz so much. But when he puts on the stocking cap and they pull out in their car, the place seems empty. I don't understand why he goes.

I write him in English. I don't ask Dad to translate it because it is personal. I send the spider strand from the coat.

I return to calling my brother by our last name. I want everything the way it was before Mr. Cedzynski came from Poland. It never goes back that way, though. I think we have to appreciate what's close to us. Stevie needs a new cap. I think I will buy him one, for at least I have my brother.

We hear no word from Łukasz Cedzynski. The snow falls. It covers the path to the creek and the BN tracks and the shores of the Great Sweetwater Sea. Pretty soon, the St. Lawrence Seaway will close for winter. The last boats have to get out of the Great Lakes. The newspaper says there's a Polish boat, the *Ziemia Białostocka*, upbound to take on flaxseed here and wheat at another grain elevator.

I don't know what it is to be a foreigner in a country. Maybe I'll learn when I go to high school. In my grade at school now, we only have seven students, Antoni Zowin, Bobby Novack, John Horyza, mostly Polish-American kids, and the high school we'll go to is big. Even this will not be like what Łukasz has experienced. The pictures in the hallway tell it. In those faces is a sadness as if the students were torn from something and are in between countries. They didn't know whether here or Poland would be better. Maybe I am foreign. I fit in here, but don't like kids like Stevie to tease me. The older girls at the high school and in the neighborhood don't have much to do with me.

Łukasz comes back on the bus, and we go to get him. He stands waiting by the Polish Club. He hugs us. He brings presents for Stevie and me. Dad, Ma, and Mr. Cedzynski talk all night. They have a bottle of vodka. The people from Chicago send their best wishes, Dad says. They listen to Polish music. Before sleep, I wonder about things. Why did Mr. Cedzynski come to Superior? Poland was an old country you talked or sang about. Now with him here, Poland has become more real to me. Our guest was living proof of something. You could look at him and know he was foreign. Maybe not understanding him was the best thing for me. While everybody around here spoke Polish, they were still Americans. But not Łukasz. He was authentic. I couldn't wait to see him in the morning.

In the middle of the night, the house grows quiet. At first it sounds like everyone's in bed. I wonder if Mr. Cedzynski is asleep. I hear voices in the vent. It must be past midnight, and someone's up after all. Stevie rolls over in his bed. Everything upstairs is quiet, just Stevie's breathing and tossing. I see the kitchen light on when I get halfway down the stairs. Dad and Mr. Cedzynski are talking. They can't hear me coming. They're going back and forth about something.

"Have a drink, Łukasz."

They have water glasses in front of them. As Mr. Cedzynski holds his glass and pours, I stand out of the light to watch. He says something in Polish. He keeps talking, then drinks the vodka. The glass teeters as he puts it down.

"Why do you want to do it?" Dad asks.

"*Jest trudno—*" it sounds like Łukasz says, then something else.

"He grew tired of living there. He had no one in Poland," Dad tells my mother. "He heard of sailors jumping ship in America. He wanted to go and be able to buy bread and shoes and not have to wait for things all the time. There was no reason to stay there, he thought."

Mr. Cedzynski turns his head like he doesn't want them to know he's torn by something inside himself. I saw him do this on the trestle.

"It'll help getting some sleep," says Mother.

"You go up, dear," Dad says. But she sits with them, checking the clock.

"I think I understand it," Dad says. "There's a tree near his parents' church where they're buried, and two roads cross and crucifixes stand along the road. The crosses are kept sheltered from the rain. Łukasz misses the stones in the roads around there. He carries a stone from home in his duffel bag."

"He has no living soul back there," says Mother.

Dad and Łukasz drink another shot. They toast the U.S. I watch Łukasz fight his tears. Then I go upstairs.

Sometimes in my room at night, the wind brushes the windows and they rattle. The snow sounds like rice against the glass. It might have been the wind that made him cry up on the trestle. I've never been away from home, so I can't say how bad a person feels. You see the sweetwater sea from upstairs. On rough, windy nights, you can hear the waves going in and out. The waves leave you wondering about everything, about human beings. If there could be a special place in the middle of a land where people were happy and not drawn back to sea like the waves, then I think things would be better for everyone. I wonder if Łukasz thinks this, too. I guess I'm happy staying in my dad's house and going to St. Adalbert's. If I lived far off, would I miss walking the shore of the lake? Would I let it draw me back? I think of the thin, silver strands on the trestle and how they hook on the walkway in the middle of their way somewhere else. They are temporary and more precious because of it. Slowly, the lake is freezing him in, I think, and I'm happy and fall back to sleep.

The next afternoon, me, Stevie, and Mr. Cedzynski go uptown on the bus. After school, he meets us by Hammerbeck's

Coffee Shop. It's fun showing him around. I let him put in the bus tokens. We walk to the wide seats in back. Mr. Cedzynski puts an arm around Stevie. Maybe Mr. Cedzynski has forgotten what he was telling himself on the trestle, I think. The bus starts and stops. The Onaway Club, Hayes Court, the sign for the Blue Star Highway go by. We pass the Red Owl Store and the college, people getting on and off.

"Mr. Cedzynski, you see the drive-in restaurant? We go there," Stevie's saying. "See that Cathedral? Sometimes, we serve Mass for the Bishop. They have services when the Knights of Columbus wear these things that look like sea uniforms they got off an old ship in a movie. You see the place in there? It used to be a plumber's. There's the Capitol Tea Room Dad took me to once …"

He's rattling on like the wind on the windows last night, and Mr. Cedzynski is nodding and smiling, pretending to understand.

I never know how close to the next corner you should pull the cord to get off. The bus slows down by the Labor Temple, Stevie talking away.

"Where would you like to go?" Mr. Cedzynski asks in Polish, but I understand because of how he says it and moves his hands.

"Guenard's," Stevie says. The owner goes to St. Francis church out by our church. Wiping his hands on his apron, he shakes everybody's hand and asks how they are when they come in.

Right away, Mr. Guenard knows Mr. Cedzynski's a foreigner. Mr. Guenard says, "*Dzień dobry*." Łukasz smiles and points to the licorice. As we eat it, he walks between us on the sidewalk. He has the stocking cap on and Dad's winter car coat. A shiny, brown sports coat Mr. Cedzynski brought from the *Ziemia Opolska* hangs down partway under the car coat. He looks lost on an American street. People stare.

When we come to a phone booth at 12th and Tower, he checks his pockets. Stevie hands him a quarter. "Mr. Cedzynski, are you calling Poland?" my brother asks.

IN THE MORNING, IT's really cold, the first morning below zero. Dad and Łukasz drive us to school. Over the door, carved in the stone entryway, it says: SZKOŁA WOJCIECHA, St. Adalbert School. Before I go in my room, I give Stevie the money for the hot lunch we have twice per school year.

I see Stevie again at noon. He wants more money. In the afternoon when the sixth and seventh grade classes study reading, I ask Sister Benitia to be excused. She lets me read from the bookshelf in back. I read and look out at the great sweetwater sea. During their conferences, Sister told Ma and Dad I was a good student but a dreamer always off in my own thoughts. The book I've been looking through is about Poland. In one of the pictures, the land is flat and green, the land trampled from the many visitors to Częstochowa. In another picture, these mountaineers, *gorali*, men who live in the High Tatras of southern Poland, are dancing. They wear colorful clothes. I think of Łukasz.

When we get home, Ma's upset. Dad is home, too. "He couldn't have just walked out and caught a bus," Dad says. "He must have gone somewhere. Maybe ... I don't know where. He left his bag."

We drive to the trestle, then down 5th Street to Belknap the way the city bus runs. We turn down Tower Avenue. We check the Kosciuszko Club on Winter Street and look in the Greyhound station. It's a big, spread-out town. Where would he go? Dad wonders. We check a few stores along Belknap and Tower. We stop by the phone booth from the day before. "He wouldn't be in a tavern, I don't think," Dad says. We drive for an hour. By the library, by Guenard's, by all of my relatives' houses. We check the whole length of Ogden Avenue, Weeks, and Banks. We go down John and up Hammond. We search Catlin Avenue and out by the oil refinery.

The docks are something if you've never seen them. The roads get bad by the docks. They're full of potholes, and you have to cross all these railroad tracks. We've got about thirty docks or more in town. From them, coal, ore, wheat, and other products are shipped. The docks have different names: Hallett Coal Dock, Farmer's Union, O&M, Great Northern 1 & 2. Dad says maybe we're the twelfth or thirteenth busiest port in the nation. In spite of the sign telling us to KEEP OUT, Dad drives up to one of the docks down by these old warehouses and fish packing places. At the bottom of huge cement elevators like grain silos is a narrow place to walk. If you stepped the wrong way, you'd fall in the water. Dad, me, and Stevie head out toward the ship. Dirty water drips from the elevators. You can hear the ship's engines. Pigeons flap around us.

"Hurry," Dad says.

The boat is huge. The smokestack and wheelhouse, the cables, the hatch covers are almost as big and high as the elevator she's leaving. Except for the name in white, the steel hull's black. Then right at the top, several thin white and green stripes run the ship's entire length and, very high up on the bow, a Polish eagle is painted in white. Its wings spread wide. Two harbor tugs move into position around her. Some sailors are hauling up the ladder, others work on deck. The hatches bang when they close them. Grain dust forms a yellow layer on the ice and snow. A sailor stares at us from above the eagle.

"We're looking for Łukasz Cedzynski!" Dad yells up.

The sailor cups his hand to his ear. Dad yells again.

The man calls to us from a long way up.

"Yes, Łukasz," Dad says. "We must speak to him. We wish to tell him something."

The sailor signals us. He disappears. The *Ziemia Białostocka* eases away from us.

"We can't stand here," Dad says. We head out to the end of the dock. The sailor returns. He hollers down above the engines. The ship is thirty feet out. He waves, shakes his head.

"Is he aboard?" Dad yells in Polish.

The man nods but hunches his shoulders as if unsure why Łukasz won't come up.

He's leaving. The tugs push the *Ziemia Białostocka* through the early season ice. The vessel leaves broken piles of it. Slowly, the tugs bring her into the harbor. We go back down the walkway, Dad hurrying Stevie who can't stop waving at the ship. "We'll watch out the entry," Dad says. "It's getting dark. Cliff will be coming over tonight."

A long, high bridge crosses the harbor and connects Superior to Duluth. Over the guardrails as Dad drives, we see the *Ziemia Białostocka* edge out far below us. In the harbor, other ships lie at anchor. You can see two miles up the St. Louis River.

"He didn't have to go. They weren't even coming to his case for four months," Dad says.

We race after him, as though we could reverse what Łukasz has done. On the other side of the bridge, we lose track of the ship where the pulpwood and coal piles are so high on Railroad Street you can't see over them. There is another bridge that ships pass under when they leave port. At the Aerial Lift Bridge, a bell will sound and the motor traffic stop as the bridge's center span rises. Dad parks on the street. We run through the cold. The Army Corps of Engineers has trucks and equipment all over. We have to zigzag around it.

The ship turns into the entry. As the bridge tender answers the *Ziemia Białostocka*'s signal, the whole center of the bridge rises into the air. Pushing the channel ice up around her, the *Ziemia Białostocka* looks like a haunted dream of Poland in the night. We hear the engines pounding and see the man above the eagle waving. He waves all the way out. We hear the ship's passing, we see her lights disappear, but we can't move, none of us, not me, Stevie, Ma, or Dad, not as long as we believe we see the lights out in the ice.

Some days later, the St. Lawrence Seaway closes for the winter. One of the last to get through, the *Ziemia Białostocka* has made it out, the Duluth paper reports. Dad checks Mr. Cedzynski's duffel bag. In it are a greeting card and five twenty-dollar bills. "*Niech cie Bòg błogosławy,*" he's written. "Let God bless you." I spend the night in my room looking at the card in his strange, foreign hand. I look from the crucifix to the rosary to the prayer book. From then on after school, I just want to come home and go upstairs to think.

Then the town freezes and there aren't any lake or ocean boats coming here. The town and the harbor just freeze over and shut down. Even the Coast Guard cutter *Woodrush* is frozen in, icebound. My life feels like it's ended. Stevie moves back into his own room. He keeps some of his things in Łukasz's duffel bag. I try writing something, a poem, but I can't even concentrate on homework from school.

One day late in winter, I come back out on the trestle. Ma'd kill me if she knew I've come here alone. Everything's sharp and white on the earth. The wind whips hard from the lake. Your eyes water and your face feels numb. I think of the times I saw him resting in Stevie's room. When I thought Mr. Cedzynski was sleeping, he was staring at the ceiling, deep in thought, hands behind his head. His dark eyes kind of dream-like, he'd mutter to himself.

Now I think about the people who've come here, about their pictures in the school hallway. Sometimes they look haunted like the dream of a ship, placeless and floating. I can hear the bridge bells ringing. What was back there that Mr. Cedzynski missed? What was in the old country that was so special he'd return to it just because of the stones in the road? I wish there could be a place where a person could forget about everything she's ever loved. That is my wish. But I know it will never be possible.

IMMIGRATION AND NATURALIZATION

An immigration officer, I have tracked down illegal aliens on ocean freighters and intercepted contraband in cars and trucks crossing our borders. As a result of these serious matters, I, Lester Stupak, have filed enough Forms I-1551 and N-400 to fill up the Federal Building in Superior, Wisconsin.

Now a difficult case arises: my wife's, whose immigration claim I can't process. All I can do is sit by her bed and hold her hand. We've agreed over the years what to do if one of us dies—and now look, my Grace is leaving for a country I know nothing about. Who are its consuls and vice-consuls that I might call to arrange her comfort?

"Lester, help," she implores when she's clearheaded from her medication and when the pain has eased. I fix her pillows, brush her folded hands with my fingers, touch her hair with my lips, wondering why, dear God, she should be dying now when we've been so happy. No prayer helps until, from a brown bottle, I pour her morphine into a plastic cup. When she's through drinking, I dab the corners of her mouth. With her at peace, I sit wondering how you give up thirty-eight years together?

"What, dear?" I hear her mutter.

"Nothing," I hear her answering herself a moment later.

"Tell me something I can get you. Just tell me what I can do to make it easier for you," I say to her.

Because she wants nothing, that's what I bring her—helplessness, nothing. I wish I could suffer for her, but God doesn't bless me this way. Her frightened, half-open eyes, pallid skin, and morphine-stained mouth; nothing, no more horrible nightmare can befall me. I watch our life diminish by day and hour. When I'm at work, I call to ask the nurse, who stays with her daytimes, whether perhaps something miraculous hasn't occurred with my wife Grace.

"Nothing." I can hear Grace herself saying it over the telephone. "Nothing."

"What? What did she say just now?" I ask.

"Nothing, Mr. Stupak. I'm sorry," the nurse says.

One evening as I pray for a miracle and over the telephone try to find a priest available to me, Grace whispers how she can't endure it anymore. More softly than my inquiries about a priest, she says, "get my medicine"; and when I've given the little larger dosage the doctor prescribes, she says, "I have to leave. Take me from here. You have to help me, Lester."

"I will. But rest. You're weak. We'll go when you're better. Do you want a priest?"

In my anguish, I pray to saints who can't help—to the Patron of Lost Causes, the Patron of Safe Voyages, the Patroness of Married Women. But a few days later before she returns to the painless dreams where she spends her time, she says it again, "You have to take me someplace far away." "I promise I will," I say. Her body is now so frail she seems made of feathers or string when I move her a little on the bed.

Over thirty-eight years, there have been miracles though, sure enough. When we were young and Catholic churches stood on every block of that city, one small miracle occurred in Milwaukee, I recall as I sit by her. Settled in our first house, I grew worried we'd be transferred. I told her, "I should quit Immigration and Naturalization."

"Where would we have to go if you took a transfer?"

"El Paso. We'd have to sell the house. I'm worried and can't sleep. I didn't want you alarmed. I should just go to college, and we can stay here."

"You've got time in with the government you'd lose. But we'll do what's best and support each other." As I sat at the kitchen table, she'd rested her cheek on my head, I remember. "Don't worry. Sleep. We'll decide tomorrow. It'll work."

The worry and frustration she'd helped me through that time—*you did, Grace, you got me through*; this was a miracle. Who knows but in its secular way it wasn't as great as what had happened spiritually to St. Theresa of Avila or St. Stephen of Hungary? *As things turned out, we never made it to the dusty Southwest, did we, Grace?"*

Other miracles blessed us, I think now. Every color and curve of her face—a miracle to me! Always. How can a person care so much for four decades? Then there are recent, occasional improvements in her health, miraculous improvements that bring the renewal of hope.

But now the slow, sad decline, now the worsening back and neck, now the frequent pleas for help—then no one but me in her room kissing her as I try to delay her passing. The miracle of her life, which was my passion, is so suddenly over that I can't believe it, and I continue to comment to her on the possibility of miracles. But none comes.

When I call at the mortuary, there is no urn, no vase, no formality, just a little plastic box. I bring her home. This is a week after her death and after the short memorial service conducted by a lay person, finally, for no priest was available that day. *And so, really, the loss of my life, too. The loss of Lester Stupak's life with his wife Grace.*

At the start of the new week, I go to the office, knowing there is immigration work to do. A Brazilian is waiting, seeking Form I-589 and information on what a *notario*, a lawyer, can and can't do. A Laotian with two children comes next to apply for the Family Unity Program. By eleven of the first day back after Grace's passing, I know I can barely finish the morning when in comes my work partner, who's been to the waterfront.

A sailor has arrived on a foreign freighter, he tells me. Clean-shaven, wearing a blue jacket and dungarees, the sailor, still a boy, makes no sense when he talks. His hands shake as we empty his pockets, pat him down, then call a translator.

"Can *anyone* understand him?" Anderson asks.

"The shipping agent from Guthrie-Hubner said they got a letter a week ago when the kid was at sea," the secretary says. "It's from his mother. Someone at Guthrie-Hubner opened it, translated it. They got him off of the ship, brought him in. He's sixteen."

"I go back," the sailor is saying. He asks Anderson and Wilson, "Do you speak Polish?" Then he prays. It is as if the sailor is writing prayers on the legal pad the secretary has given him. "I go back," he keeps saying, scribbling with a pencil. "You mail for me?" he asks me. The address is: Dorota Fierek at *ul. Zniwo* Gdańsk, Poland. I place it in my pocket.

"He wants a taxi back to his ship," Anderson says.

"Oh no," says Wilson, "you can't go. Government police are looking for you in Gdańsk. You'll be arrested. You're a protestor. You can't return to the *Ziemia Chelmińska*. She's sailing for Poland the day after."

"Yes, return to Poland," says the sailor, whose blond hair falls across his forehead. Black eyebrows above the tired eyes contrast with his hair and with the face flushed with worry and sorrow. All over in Poland, there have been strikes: textile workers, coal miners, shipyard workers. The kid has been seen marching. I try to get the sailor's crying out of my head. It sounds like crying in every INS office on our floor—Vietnamese, Cambodians, Guatemalans—sounds like it in the halls, at the vending machines, in the lavatory. At the elevator, I remember the Pole's letter. I mail it, then forget what's happened.

Everywhere at home, however, I am reminded of the comings and goings of asylum seekers. From Grace's window, I see a harbor and western terminus of Lake Superior and the Great

Lakes. Ocean freighters load flax for Greece, heavy equipment for Saudi Arabia, wheat for the Soviet Union, corn, sunflower seeds, cement, even scrap metal for South Korea. Grain and cement dust rise above the gray docks, the terminals, the city. Looking out, I'm reminded of émigrés wishing to leave an old country and stay in a new one. Sailors, illegals, wander the docks at night, waiting for their ships to return so they will have friends to talk to. My wife Grace has gone, and I have no one to talk to. I think if I don't do something to find her, I'll have to sit here with my head on the kitchen table, not eating or sleeping until someone, until Grace, comes. At nine, at nightfall, afraid to be alone in the house, I leave for a place I know.

On the docks, the security guard at Harvest States Elevator lets me pass. I turn toward the harbor slip, park the car. Grain silos tower overhead. Back to back, two ocean ships can load simultaneously at each dock, though the docks are silent tonight. Above the silos' vent fans, seamen have painted "*Belle Etoile*12/19/82," "*Senator of Athens* 3/4/85," "M/S [motor ship] *Baronia*," and the name of a vessel that was in late last fall, *Ziemia Białostocka*." Records of a visit to a grain terminal.

In the middle of the night, a lake freighter glides by. "Do you remember, Grace, we were going to fix up the house when I retired?" I whisper. Thinking of her, I put my hand to my chest, to my heart. As I do, I notice someone moving. There. Outside.

Turning on the headlights, I see another hand rise to another heart, see a sailor's blue jacket. Frightened, he hurries out of view, leaving me to remember his face in the dark as the rain starts, leaving me to recall how bleak and gray life has been for so long. When she got sick, the room turned gray, the sky turned gray. While I comforted her, it'd rained for two years, for three years. She'd snatch at the air with curled hands, the result of the morphine. Sometimes when I asked, "Grace, what is it?", she'd say, "Nothing."

"We'll take the trips we never took before. We'll fix the house nice," I whisper to her when I think I hear her crying. But outside there. Again. Now a tapping on the passenger-side window. The rain on the glass washes away the face that was there.

"Who are you?" I call through the window. "What do you want with me? Your ship's gone to another dock. You were to have stayed in a hotel."

Rain, the blue lights of the dashboard, the name and time of ships' visits written in paint on a grain terminal.

He taps again.

Slowly, he unbuttons his shirt. His youthful hand is lost beneath the jacket and the shirt. Lonely at heart, he wants me to look through the window at him. He wants me to see his heart.

"I've lost someone," I whisper, as I place my hand to my chest. A whistle comes from off in the harbor. So often I've heard the ships. He has only himself here in America. He was to have stayed in a seaman's hotel a few blocks away.

Through the rain, I see him moving closer. I see the hand pressed to the bare heart. I run my fingers across the inside of the window to his heart. "What is it you want? I've lost someone. It's nighttime."

He can't understand. He's looking for asylum and will have to cross the border with me, the representative of INS. If he does, I will explain to him in the car in the shadow of the silos just what has happened here tonight and why he can't return home. A "Request for Asylum," a form I-589—he will need this signed by Agent-in-Charge Stupak.

"Please, *pleace*," he's saying, "give me a ride from the rain."

I place my hand on the window, hold my hand to the glass so close to him. Nearly touching his heart, I see now in the passenger side window that I've become an old man who's returned so many people to the countries they've fled, sent them to nowhere, to nothing, have had this power. How thin the glass of a window! Somehow, the face I see in the reflection of the car window has sunken over the years, presenting an odd collection of angles to asylum seekers who never knew how to look on the face of nothing. How often I've told good people that evidence for wanting to leave their home country was insufficient. They'd sit there fearfully, expectantly. When others asked, "Is it hard to remain in America?", I'd point to the government pamphlet that read: YES, THERE ARE NO QUICK AND EASY WAYS TO OBTAIN ASYLUM STATUS. Remembering those whom I've denied asylum over forty years has given me heart problems.

Now Grace has gone away, and I'm crying as I look for her reflection in the car window. The INS agent reflected in the glass offers little consolation to the weary traveler looking to him for asylum. "Here," I say to the boy. "Here is your Form I-589, your Request for Asylum." I try to present it to him, but there's no way to cross this border until I open the door and unlock my heart to him.

"Come in. Yes," I say to him.

When he sits beside me, we look at each other in the blue light. He's crossed the ocean and now, here in America, a stranger asks to hold him. "Come. Sit with me just a moment. Please," I say. I reach for his hand.

He desires this, too.

We hold each other, the Agent-in-Charge and the young seaman, and no one ever needs to know how it is to be so lonely that a man will want to hold a boy in his arms in a parked car on a rainy night, maybe kissing him on the forehead before sending him out again into the sea of darkness we live in.

ENGLISH AS A SECOND LANGUAGE

In my class that semester were a student from Laos, who'd been here five years; a student from Hong Kong, who preferred to be called "Andy"; three from Japan, Mr. Ishida, Mr. Takahashi, and Miss Tanigawa; and a student from Vietnam, who disrupted things. Actually, Miss Nguyen caused two disturbances.

The less serious disruption occurred one day when she read from the class workbook. The others looked up, for I was speaking to them and especially to Mr. Ishida about subject-verb agreement when Miss Nguyen began reading aloud. Maybe she was reading the tale of the bull and the lion, I don't recall. I do remember the black hair hanging about her face, so that we couldn't see her looking at the words. But we could hear her soft voice. She was so busy she paid no attention to us, just kept reading.

"Miss Nguyen, please!" I said.

"Teacher?" she asked, looking up.

It was customary in Vietnam, I'd learned, to call the instructor this. I'd been in her country in 1965. We'd stopped in Japan and Okinawa, too, which was useful to me as a teacher. When I served in Vietnam, I thought I'd been pronouncing "Nguyen" properly. I remember saying Nguyen Cao Ky when he was premier of South Vietnam.

Now when I pronounced it "Nooyen," she said "Nyen," so that we agreed I should stop trying.

"Thanh," she said. I didn't understand what she rattled off. "Speak slower," I said. "Say slowly what you wish to say."

"You should call me Thanh," she said.

So that was the reading incident near the start of the semester in September. The second disturbance occurred later as the students' English improved slightly. Miss Nguyen, who was thirty-eight or thirty-nine years old now, was doing okay. We'd been through subject-verb agreement, transitions between sentences, and pronoun reference errors, and we'd even written one or two paragraphs about ourselves from which I'd found out that "Andy" feared the Chinese coming to Hong Kong in 1997, that Chong Vang, who wore a strand of yarn about his wrist, had once narrowly escaped the Viet Cong, and that Masanori Ishida deplored the easy life of American students vis-á-vis their Japanese counterparts. In a paper written in pencil, Miss Nguyen told me she'd hoped to go to college in Saigon, but had failed an important exam and had ended up working two years as a secretary in Saigon City Hall.

"You must explain what you mean. I don't understand," I said. When I looked out the window, I saw construction work all over the campus.

"I doan know, Teacher," she said. She smiled. She wore colorful dresses with dark greens and bright yellows like the jungle. Her hair was black. The frames of her glasses were black. Half the time, I didn't understand her.

The Japanese were easier to decipher. Usually, I just smiled back at them. Sometimes, it's easier to smile than to listen. When you're forty-six years old and going nowhere in life, why do you have to do anything you don't want to do? Why listen at all? The war was over. We'd lost in Vietnam. Why was Miss Nguyen taking English 100? The war was done, I thought again.

I was nineteen when they'd brought in the prisoners. Wearing a helmet with a white cross taped on the top, I would run out to a helicopter landing zone and stand with my arms raised in a "Y." Sometimes, the door gunner would shove the prisoners out of the helicopter. Not so much as waving to me, the pilot and his door gunner would take off into the sky, leaving the blindfolded men with us. They were dressed in black pants and shirts. With their hands tied behind their backs, I'd lead them in a line to the motor pool. At first, the guys harassed them until the lieutenant put a halt to it.

"Teacher!" Miss Nguyen said. I hadn't looked at the paper she and the others were writing in class. The topic was, "What Was the Nicest Thing Anyone Ever Did for You?"

"Yes, this is good," I said. I leaned over Thanh Nguyen's desk. She'd written four short paragraphs. I still have her paper. I remember I'd kicked one of the prisoners. They were scared. Maybe they were innocent peasants, not VC at all. This one had started talking back to me. I kicked him. I stuffed a rag in his mouth. Miss Thanh Nguyen's paper read:

"I was born, grew up in a big family. So my mother and my oldest sister had worked very hard every day to take care all of us. The seven children lived in the same house until the one who found a job and left and so on for the rest.

The thing that I have never forgotten is that my mother is the best mother of ours. She helped, cared, and comforted when we needed her. I remember the evenings after school, we ran through miles of rice field and got home with starving stomach, the hot meals were there for us. My mother had saved from pennies to nickels just for the children's food and school. She encouraged us to study every day and night. She told us that she would like to see us become good person in community.

And one thing more I haven't forgotten was how the last minutes my brother and I would say to my mother for leaving the native country. He came in out of the jungle. She walked along with us to the local bus station. As I got on the bus, my brother look around. She still stood on the road with her tears. She waited to wave her hand to say good bye forever. I left on the bus. My brother—"

"Miss Nguyen. This is good," I said. "But look here in line two ... you need an 'of.' Can you see?"

As I was talking to her, I remembered how I'd kicked the prisoner as he was falling to the ground in the motor pool, kicked him in the same ear as I was talking to her in.

"Miss Nguyen?"

"Teacher?"

"It's this line about your mother. It's too confusing. Also, look at this other sentence. 'The thing that I have never forgotten that my mother is the best mother of ours.'" Let's change the thing, change the whole country, I thought. "Don't think Vietnamese, Miss Thanh. Think English ..."

I began to write with her pencil. She was hidden behind her black hair and her black eyes. I always knew when VC were outside of the perimeter. Thanh Nguyen must've been young, hidden there in the jungle, too, I thought. "Let's write it this way. 'I have never forgotten the beauty and kindness of my mother.' Don't you see it's clearer?" I went through more sentences, adding an ending or a word. It must have been very hard for her to leave Vietnam, I thought. She was not so bad. She was smiling, Thanh Nguyen.

I could feel her beside me and hear her breathing. Miss Tanigawa and Mr. Ishida were looking at us. "I'll just add this 's,'" I said. I only thought Miss Nguyen had a cold from the autumn weather. But the rest of the students were looking at us—from Japan, from Laos and Hong Kong, which in five years was to revert to China. They'd left their desks and their papers. She was hiding something. I could feel her sobs as she crossed her arms and hid behind her hair so that I wouldn't see. It didn't matter to her that the others watched. "*Ma mère, ma mère*," she was whispering.

"Miss Nguyen, do you miss her? Is that why? Is it how I've changed your essay?"

I was forty-six, I realized again, and going nowhere ... a

Westerner. I didn't need to listen. I gave her the pencil. I could have told her about my mother, who was gone now. I used to write my mother from Vietnam. She died while I was there.

I went to the blackboard. Thanh Nguyen still hid behind her hair in the jungle. I couldn't see her ear because of her hair. This one had talked back to me. It was an incident of war. I stared out at the campus and the city at the Head of the Lakes. When they were drinking together, some guys at the Vets Center still called them "Gooks." It had been an incident of war with the prisoner, the rag in his mouth, my kicking him and all. Twenty-seven years later, the guys at the Vets Center were still calling them names.

"*Mam*," Mr. Vang said very softly.

"Write it down," I said.

"Our word for mother," he said. He wrote it on the board.

"*Ma ma*," said Mr.Chi-Hanh Tse. He spoke it in Chinese.

"*Okâsan*," said the two Japanese, Mr. Ishida and Mr. Taka-hashi.

"Mother?" I said. "Is that what it means?"

"Write it down," they said.

I put it on the board.

"How you say it in colloquial *Englash*?" Miss Tanigawa asked.

"Mom or Ma," I said.

"Can you write it for us?"

I put this up, too.

"Don't anyone erase the board once I leave," I said. "Leave the words here for a while." I looked out the window again. The Red Cross had delivered a message by the same copter I'd signaled down with a white cross on my helmet and with my arms forming a "Y." My news came with the new prison-ers. "Here!" the machine gunner had yelled as he pushed out six VC. Blindfolded, they'd started running. The draft from the helicopter blades blew their hair about. "Here!" He was handing it to me, a telegram from my sister. "Thanks," I said. I stepped back, gave the pilot the signal to take off. Some other guys rounded up the prisoners. It was mail for me. I was happy, an unexpected mail call: "Ma died … Funeral Sat.," it read. "Can you come?"

Twenty-seven years ago, I read it. I was in South Vietnam thinking of Ma. She'd died. I hadn't been there. Now someone else was thinking of home. Now someone was replacing me. I didn't mean it about your mother, Thanh, I thought. I didn't mean changing your words. "Leave it," I said. "Leave the lines in your papers as they are and go home. All of you. They're pretty good sentences … pretty good papers. All of yours are."

Never able to pronounce my name right, a Polish name, they said, "Thank you, Mr. Vanka-wicz." They walked out slowly, Miss Nguyen going back into the jungle.

Outside, some university workers were ripping up the sidewalks. There was always work going on. I watched them from the window. It was getting late in the day. I wrote on the board, PLEASE SAVE THIS. I'd wait up all night in the room to keep the janitors away from it if I had to. I'd make sure of it. Mr. Ishida had written the word in Japanese script, then he'd written, *Okâsan*, Mother.

Ma mére, I thought, saying it the way Thanh Nguyen would say it. I sat a long time dreaming of my mom and of the Polish word for mother, *matka*. It was already dark when I began recopying our words on the blackboard, drawing them the way we'd done it. In Japanese and Vietnamese, in Chinese, Hmong, and Polish, there are many words for mother. "*Matka Boska*" is "Mother of God." I kept writing it on the board. Then the door opened, and in came the night-school students, local kids with their own language for what is precious.

THE CASE FOR BREAD AND SAUSAGE

The priest's housekeeper sits him in a lawn chair on the rectory's front porch. To keep him warm, she's dressed him in a car coat and watch cap, then ducked into the rectory to worry and pace. If you're brave enough to ride past on your bicycle, you see Father helpless from the stroke, Lu, the housekeeper, watching over him through the picture window. Maybe he waves or says something you can't understand. Then he starts crying. Sad Father Nowak will cry for hours if no one comes to see him.

Walter and I are thirteen. Walter says "hello" to the people passing us on their way to church.

It's no fun for us to serve Mass for the priests who replace Father Nowak, especially when we know that later Father will be out here on this cool June morning, the Feast of the Sacred Heart, and we'll have to pretend not to see him. Who wouldn't be sad seeing him like this?

Sometimes, Father calls to us, thinking that we've come to help him. If he could be like he once was, if only an angel could whisper, "This is St. Adalbert's church. Do you remember how you came here from Toledo long ago?", then we'd feel better.

"We can't go home later," Walter says, breaking the bad news to me when we get to church. "Lu called my ma. We're serving Mass out in the country. We might not eat till after the twin-bill. We're serving a double-header, the Mass right now, then the Mass later."

"I've got things to do," I say.

Walter isn't happy either.

After we walk down the aisle between the pews of old women, we try to look sincere in our bows to the altar. Genuflecting before the Communion railing, we cross ourselves and head for the sacristy.

We aren't sure what's going on in there. Then we hear this guy call out, "Help me. I've had too much wine." Appearing from the shadows, we see a thing so big we could imagine it in a fairy tale, like the giant in "Jack and the Beanstalk." Whatever it is has dark hair so wavy that it looks like his head is balancing the marks you see over Spanish words. The eyes in the red face look like they're accustomed to sizing up people for what the owner of the eyes can get from them. The rest of him—he is part shadow, part reality—I can't describe, except to say that moving is hard for him and is accompanied by many groans. To help him dress for the altar, Walter and I yank on the chasuble in order to get it over his neck. In the censer used for the Benediction of the Blessed Sacrament, the "Jack and the Beanstalk" monster has been putting out his cigarettes.

When he grunts once or twice and walks out onto the altar with us, he says, "*In nomine Patris, et Filii et Spiritus Sancti.* Amen." The slurred words sound like "*Shpiritus Shancti.*"

By the "Confiteor," I'm so hungry I forget the priest. This hunger comes because we can't eat before receiving Communion. I get hungrier during the "Kyrie" and the "Glory Be."

When the priest says, "*Corpus Domini nostri Jesu Christi—*" which his drunkenness turns into, "*Corpush Domini noshtri,*" Walter and I know we'll be fed a little at least. This is what I mean by the Case for Bread and Sausage: I think that the wheat of the Blessed Sacrament can satisfy our hunger. Maybe this can be said of sausage as well. When the priest gives us Communion, he says, "Have I got a hangover!"

Lu has given us a lunch to take to the Danbury mission. It is a fifty-mile trip to there. It is known as a mission because there aren't enough parishioners for a priest to be assigned full time. During our first Mass of the day, the visiting priest has had a hard time holding the Host aloft. I guess he was so hungover that his hands shook. Now he squeezes himself into Father Nowak's Ford Fairlane. With the good smells in the car, I think of what might be in the box of food Lu's prepared for us. The problem is the priest smells these things, too. Walter and I dream of bread and sausage, of pie and cake.

During the "Introit" at the mission, I whisper, "Walter, I'm starved." As if to tempt us, the Latin words the priest says sound like something you'd have for breakfast or dessert. "*Dominus vobiscum*" sounds like "*Dominus Nabisco*," "*Oremus* ... Oreos."

Then the priest says, "Lord, I'm not worthy that Thou shouldst come under my roof."

Judging from the looks on the worshippers' faces, they're as starved as we are. There are twenty faithful people in the six pews. When I hold the gold plate, the paten, under their chins to catch any blessed crumbs that might fall, they seem to long for the Eucharist in a way that Walter and me don't understand. What my grandma or my neighbors get from Communion is a mystery, perhaps because they've come from the old country.

Thankfully, the priest zips us through the "Final Prayers," the "Blessing," and the "Last Gospel." With everyone gone home, I think he'll allow us to eat. Before he hands us one of the cruets used during Mass, he enjoys another sip of altar wine from it. Still in his vestments, he walks behind the mission for a cigarette.

"Let's see what Lu's packed."

"The box still feels warm," Walter says, "but I can't let us open it yet."

"Why? The first of the seven Corporal Works of Mercy is To Feed the Hungry."

"No matter. We can't look inside," Walter says.

"You sound like you're nuts. The heck with the Danbury mission," I tell him. "What kind of priest doesn't care about other people? He's so fat he blocked the tabernacle from view."

Walter won't give in.

"Help me out of this outfit," the priest says when he returns.

We let him place the vestments in the trunk of the car. After he's held out his hands for me to pour water over them from the other cruet, the priest says, "Move that food up here."

Gunning the car, he starts down the road.

"Father," Walter says from where we're sitting in back, but the priest doesn't hear him. Admiring a sandwich, he says, "My favorite. When I was in the seminary, I knew the wrestlers that came through town. Haystacks Calhoun, Baron Von Raschke. I thought I had a vocation that way." Tearing off the crust which he sets on the dashboard, he bites into the sandwich. Tossing the remaining bread, he grabs another sandwich. "I thought hard about a pro wrestling vocation."

By now, Walter regrets keeping us from eating. I think of Father Nowak's suffering, of how the new priest must lie to his parishioners about everything.

"I'm hungry!" he says as I sink deeper into the back seat. Gnawing a carrot or a radish, he tosses some of it out the window, then digs into the sausages. He doesn't finish until he's eaten six bratwurst, the ring baloney, five sandwiches, and whatever else is in there, eats everything, every last crumb.

"Can we have those crusts, Father?" Walter asks.

"They might have dust on them from the dashboard. Here. Eat up."

It's important to respect a priest. Our parents would say, "*Ażwas, zjadaw chleba—w aniolow przerobi* ... You lowly eaters of bread will be made into angels." That's no comfort, not when we're lowly eaters. Walter puts one crust in his shirt pocket. But the thought of a crust of bread offers me no consolation. Maybe this is how the Host feeds our spirit—by making us long for It. Maybe the Eucharist means longing. I've heard Mrs. Dzikon-ski, a Displaced Person from Poland, say that when her family passed through Russia, she'd lost hope of seeing bread again. I've read that our ancestors came to America "for bread, *za chlebem.*" If I drop a piece of bread at home, when I pick it up, Ma makes me kiss it. I think I know now why Jesus went forty days and nights without food and why Father Nowak spent forty years at St. Adalbert's church in our service. They wanted us to be saved. I think this is why Father cries so often. He thinks he's failed.

"Now look," says the priest. His thick fingers reach for the dessert I forgot Lu put in there. Wiping his mouth with his fingers, he says, "You share what's left. The Lord be with you."

We see nothing in the box but a cardboard bottom. The priest has eaten his way back to town. Seeing he's behind schedule on something, he drops us off at the rectory and peels out in Father's car. He startles Father Nowak on the front porch where Lu has parked him in his wheelchair with an army blanket over his shoulders.

Not wanting to see our priest in his condition, Walter and I yell, "Go! Run!" and start our getaway for home and our mothers' cooking. But we stop after a few steps because Father is saying he's hungry.

"So are we," we tell him, Walter pulling the crust from his pocket.

When we go up on the porch to feed him bits of the crust, Father Nowak calms down. Because we've come to him despite his sadness and confusion, maybe he senses we will someday be good men. Lu can't believe the change in Father Nowak until my pal and I point to the crumbs of wheat bread on Father's car coat and tell Lu through the window that, lowly eaters of bread, we're feeding the hungry.

REPORT OF THE GUARDIAN OF THE SICK

I

Al Dziedzic's son survived Vietnam by telling himself that things would be better when he got home. Now that he was back in Superior, Wisconsin, the old man and his son had begun arguing, this time over how to clean the claw-footed bathtub. On his knees, Pete had used Comet and a washcloth as he scrubbed, yet the old man—head buzzing in the bathroom steam—still claimed to see rings bigger than the rings of Pluto near the bottom of the tub.

"Saturn's the planet with rings, not Pluto," said his son, kneeling beside the toilet. He'd been discharged from the Marine Corps and home three weeks, long enough to grow out his hair, which was drying in a towel twisted into a turban. "It's shadowy in here, but your eyes have gone bad if you can't see I cleaned it."

His father had begun to shrink, Pete noticed. To support his back, the old man had to strap himself into a beige-colored lady's corset, which he wore over his T-shirt. Grabbing a light-bulb from the kitchen cabinet, then limping back, Al Dziedzic stood on the chair he'd lugged in earlier. Fumbling with the screws holding the glass globe to the bathroom ceiling, he unscrewed the bulb, replaced it with a 100-watt bulb.

"See them rings of Pluto in the bright light?" Al asked. "Look at the dirt in the tub. It ain't cleaned to my specifications."

"Pass the Comet. You're right," said Pete. To please him, he sprinkled cleanser again, ran the water, swished it around.

A half-hour before he was to meet the guys for a night on the town, and here he was in pajamas, the marine ex-corporal, yellow turban unwinding so he couldn't see what he was rinsing. It was embarrassing for a war veteran not to pass bathtub inspection and to have the general sashaying around in a corset.

When Al went into the living room, Mrs. Dziedzic whispered, "I'll do the tub for you later, Pete. Your dad's back's been bothering him." As she put away the supper dishes, she called to her husband, "You rest out there, honey. You have to work."

It's not his back, Pete thought, but me making him miserable. The doctor might be right about Al developing osteoporosis in addition to emphysema, but it was worse than that. Pete knew the old man had mental problems revolving around *him*. When he'd missed Mass a few weeks earlier, the old man had gotten riled up. When he said he hated the Chmielewski Brothers' polka show on Channel 6, the old man had gotten even angrier. There were a lot of things Al disliked about his son, including that he was a wise guy. Whenever Al had been asked at The Warsaw Tavern when his pride and joy was returning from Vietnam, he'd sipped from his bowl of beer, ordered three pigs' feet, and grumbled, "He's coming in the depth of winter." He'd say the last part in Polish, "*w pelni zimy*."

But this, too, should be remembered: Al going to Mass before work to pray for Pete; Al, heart sinking, thinking of his boy and praying when he read in the newspaper of the fighting near Da Nang.

Still, the war the old man had started long ago was worsening now that Pete had returned. If it wasn't the old bathtub that would never sparkle, the stringy moustache the silly kid was growing, or the two teeth he'd lost in a fight, then it was the used car Al thought his son shouldn't have bought. The Rambler stood beside the garage in a spot Pete had shoveled. The electrical cord from the tank heater under the hood connected to an extension cord he'd plugged into a garage outlet. The car would never start in frigid weather without the heater to warm the engine block.

His own car parked in the garage, rear bumper sticker reading "YOU BETCHA YOUR DUPA I'M POLISH," Al Dziedzic kept telling Pete in the three weeks he'd been back from Vietnam via Camp Pendleton, California, "It's a waste of electricity having the car plugged in."

"I'll need reliable wheels if I get a job," Pete had said.

"Apply at the flour mill. There's no place to plug in a car down there. You don't need a car. You can walk to work."

"I tol' you I'm not working at the mill. I'll pay you for the electricity I use for the tank heater," Pete said, but what he offered was not enough to calm the wasps in the laborer's head. Since his son had been discharged from the Marine Corps, Al Dziedzic had begun calling him "*Dupa*, ass."

Eighteen years ago he'd started in on Pete after the parish priest, a 160 lifetime-average bowler, had told Al, "If you wanted to be happy, you should have followed a spiritual vocation like I did. No wife, no children."

"That ain't a comfort," Al had replied.

Father's words running through his head on a Knights of Columbus League bowling night, Al had missed a 7-10 split. There went the league title, there went the trophy for the Polish parish. He was still teased about it. Not only the priest, but the Dziedzic kids themselves were to blame for putting the kibosh on a life of fun. Sure, after he'd married, Al still had his yearly bowling banquet and his weekly league bowling night to anticipate, but now he also had a wife, then two children, then a workingman's house to care for. He'd once been free, though. If days were long working outside of Minot, North Dakota, or Cass Lake, Minnesota, on the Great Northern section crew, the nights in town—before he'd married Wanda—were filled with drinking and dancing. He never thought he'd be trapped with a wife and kids.

Destiny for joyless Al Dziedzic was the dust on his work clothes, the dust on the packing floor of the flour mill, the dust in the water of the slip beside the mill. Sometimes Wanda was dust. The kid was dust, like the time Al had asked Pete, home on leave from the service, to wear his uniform and drop by the boiler room. The guys during lunch break would be impressed with Al's son in his forest green uniform with the scarlet chevrons. The kid never showed up while Al ate his meat sandwich, finished his windmill cookies, closed the lunch bucket. But there was also this to remember: Al on the packing floor talking about Pete. No matter how he had it in for him, sometimes Al couldn't help but brag about his son when he was away. The old man was mixed up. Then two weeks ago, as if to spite him, the kid had left out his partial plate at the breakfast table.

"There are only two teeth in front missing. They made me false ones in Vietnam."

"What happened? Where?" Wanda gasped.

"This is what war is like, Ma."

Al removed his own choppers to lord it over his son. "You make your bed, you lay in it," he said

Al, the bitter and relentless one: Wanda cut his hair with electric clippers, washed his blue work shirts, packed his lunch bucket, sent him off to work with a kiss. When the guys gathered in the boiler room, Al, for forty years now sitting in his white miller's cap, would open his lunch bucket to see which tidbit Wanda had surprised him with. Once, he'd found a wad of chewing tobacco in an Eddie's Snoball. Thereafter, she bought him Hostess products, Twinkies and the like.

For Pete's part, he'd been getting an education from all of this. He was being home schooled. In fact, he was nearing the Ph.D. level of home schooling. He'd heard the academic term from his mother. She'd completed a two-year associate's degree at the college in Superior. She'd also gotten a certificate in "The Palmer Method of Muscular Movement Business Writing."

According to her diploma, she was qualified "to execute successfully this system of Business Penmanship." Though she had two years of higher education, she still called the credential her college professors had a "Ph—" degree.

"What you're saying sounds like an acid neutralizer. You forget the 'D.' Ph.D., Ma. Remember when I'd go to the store? Your grocery lists read 'Buy titbit for Dad.' That's wrong, too. It's tidbit," Pete said, feeling it was high time for him to do some correcting around here. If, when he was younger, he'd sneaked a Lucky Strike from Al or disrespected the nuns, he'd have been corrected pronto by the guy who'd left the railroad for the flour mill in Superior and who was now downstairs complaining, "This corset'll squeeze me and kill me."

"Come up here. I'll tighten it good for you," Pete said as he looked through his discharge papers. Now with the temperature eight below zero in northern Wisconsin, he was out of cigarettes, his hair was damp, and the general was bugging him about things beyond his control. Even Wanda said the bathtub would never look new. At least he was through with the Marine Corps. On second thought, today's temperature at Camp Pendleton might be seventy degrees, he thought.

II

When he needed to escape the old man, Pete attended Happy Hour, which runs from 8-9:30 in the morning at Hudy's Polish Palace, then resumes for two hours at 4 o'clock, though there's little to be happy about during a Superior, Wisconsin, winter. Say you're looking for Ted Wierzynski, Bernie Gunski, or Joe Novack. By the time you inquire about them at Hudy's, they'll generally be heading around the horn for cocktails at other fine East End establishments, the Warsaw Tavern perhaps. If you leave your neighborhood to have a beer in every Tower Avenue bar in the uptown three miles away, that is called the "Death March." Few return to a tavern for two or three days after a Death March. Going around the horn in East End with its four bars takes less out of the drinker than the Death March through the bars uptown. Knowing this, what puzzled Pete as he hurried through the cold to Hudy's Polish Palace was where his father had gotten a corset. What other East End man wore a foundation garment? Next his old man would sport a bra, Pete chuckled.

Standing before the "*Na Zdrowie*" sign, a toast meaning "to drink to somebody's health," "Hudy" Hudacek was finishing a bag of peanuts. A line of retired laborers slumped at the bar.

"How's your nuts, Hudy?" Pete asked.

"Salty. How's urine?" Hudy said.

"The way you like 'em. I wish I was in California."

"How's your dad?"

"*Nie ma Ojca.*"

"Oh, Al's all right," Hudy said. "Sure you have a Dad. You can't deny that."

"Beer for all, Hudy, courtesy of the USMC."

In a booth, two of Pete's friends were preparing to join the Polish Club uptown. No one but old people—dads, uncles, and grandfathers—did this. "We'll join it for a joke," Ted Wierzynski was saying.

"You walk here in the cold, Pete?" Bernie Gunski asked.

"Pete's the one that don't own a car."

"I do. Look by my old man's garage. Whose car do you suppose that is? A friend of mine drove it there for me when I bought it. Pretty soon I'll get a driver's license. Right now, I practice driving in a spot I cleared. When the old man is at work, I inch the car forward and backward to get the hang of it. I've driven fifteen inches, 1¼ feet. I figured out how to work the lights, too. Ma doesn't dare tell Al about me sitting out there practicing in the cold."

"You won't have to worry about extra mileage driving her

like that," Bernie Gunski said. "You'll go six feet this year."

"It's plugged in and the engine turns over. I'll buy you guys a round," Pete said.

"We need a polka," Mr. Pogozalski said.

"You'll wreck Happy Hour," Pete said. "Play your polkas when we're not here."

"Let him listen to the jukebox. We have something else to do," Ted said.

"She's Too Fat Polka" was playing now. Outside, beyond the glare of the "*Na Zdrowie*" signs at other bars in the two-block East End business district, they could see the arch over Fifth Street the ore dock makes. They could see Eddie Meyer's TV-Radio Repair, Sully's Café, the windows iced over. A train rolled toward the flour mill. "I had another fight with the old man."

"Never mind that. Hand me a beer, Pete. Gunner's getting really stinko."

"No wonder Al can't breathe working in flour dust. He walks around eight hours a night with a vacuum machine blowing dust off of the motors. That's what they call it at the flour mill, blowing motors. It sounds like a crime against nature."

"I'd never settle for a job like that."

"Are we here?" Gunner mumbled.

"You know what Al calls me? No matter what I do, graduate from high school, join the Corps, build a birdbath, cut the lawn, it's 'Bozo.' Did Bozo wash the car today? Did Bozo do this or that?' A bozo's a clown that sits above a tank of water and yells at people to throw a ball at a target and dunk him. Well, I'm high and dry, Al. This Bozo ain't wet yet. While I was drying my hair at home, I decided I'm reenlisting. I'm going back in the Corps and taking the Rambler. Maybe I'll have a sergeant's stripes the next time we meet, if we ever do."

"Seven beers are too many to drink in an hour," Gunski was saying.

"Some night we'll make it fourteen in an hour," Pete said.

III

When applying for membership in the Kosciuszko Fraternal Lodge of Superior, you follow certain procedures. You fill out the application form. During the waiting period, regular Kosciuszko members sit in the dance hall upstairs while you sit in the bar downstairs. The members are following the Order of Business listed in the club's *Constitution and By-Laws*. The Introduction of Applicants for Membership comes late in a meeting after the Treasurer's Report. Tonight, the twenty lodge brothers who showed up scraped their overshoes on the floor, complained about the bitter cold.

The dance hall smelled like cabbage and cigarette butts. A Polish flag hung on the wall. Dr. Kielbasa, The Wally Na Zdrowie Trio, and The World's Most Dangerous Polka Band had recently held a Battle of the Bands. Aftershocks were still felt. After Mass at the Polish and Slovak churches—and all day and night in the downstairs bar—people talked about how Wally Na Zdrowie had taken the Polish Club by storm with his hit "I'm from Planet Polka."

At a table before crossed Polish and American flags, Mr. Grymala, the lodge president, said, "Rise please!" when the sergeant-at-arms led the trio of applicants into the hall.

"Citizens, raise your right hands," the vice president said to them, then read from the *Constitution*: "I call on you before God and before the entire Thaddeus Kosciuszko Society to reply to the following truthfully, for if it should later develop that your statement was made not in accordance with truth, you will be expelled with the loss of all rights and privileges. What are your names?"

"Pete Dziedzic, Ted Wierzynski, Bernard Gunski."

"Ages?"

"Twenty-two."

"Nationality?"

"Polish-American."

"In good health?"

"Yes."

"Do you promise to abide by the by-laws and constitution of the Thaddeus Kosciuszko Lodge, so help me God?"

"Yes."

To commemorate the occasion, Mr. Grymala gave them a Wally Na Zdrowie phonograph album. On the cover was a photo of Wally in a smoky dance hall, one hand on the keys of his accordion, the other pointing to a group of hippies with granny glasses and long hair. "Polka or Get Out!" the words above the photo said.

When new lodge brothers are taken in, applause will ring through an old hall. Seeing the joy in the workingmen's faces, the boys had sobered up. They swore never again to disparage polka music. When the applause died, Mr. Grymala nodded to the guardian of the sick for his report.

"On 12/10," Joe Dembroski, the sick director, said, reading from a sheet of paper, "I visited Frank Rozowski at St. Francis Nursing Home. He's eighty. He sends a hello to us. The next day, I visited George Ham. He slumps in a wheelchair. When English don't work, I try speaking Polish. He's in pain, so I leave him a card for the nurses to read him. I went on 12/11 to see Ed Budnick at his house. He's bothered by rheumatism. I'm sad about your pa, Pete. I visited there, too, before you got home. He's sick with his lung and his back. I don't know why he works at the flour mill anymore. Al will be proud of you tonight."

"Hooray for Pete and the boys," the members said.

"Your ma and dad, when you were in Vietnam, they didn't want you knowing he was missing work."

"He's crabby. What's wrong with him now? Aren't his dues paid?"

"He could never get here to pay them when you were

gone," Mr. Grymala said. "June was the last time. He was in bad shape."

Pete calculated that, in June, he'd been wading through road dust that rose to the tops of his boots. The fine dust veiled the blistering sun, and his friends at home were writing him about the cool summer. According to Mr. Grymala, Al had been operated on twice during that period. No one had told Pete about Al Dziedzic, the bowling star, and his misery.

"I know it's not much of a sick benefit. Same as in 1928 when the lodge started," the guardian of the sick was saying.

"I'll tell the old man about it."

The members shuffled about, coughed. The boys saluted the Polish flag. Pete heard the president pound his gavel, heard the low voices talking about Al's sickness, heard the jukebox playing. "Are there additions or corrections to the Report of the Guardian of the Sick?" Mr. Grymala was asking.

IV

The car was stiff. It wouldn't move when Ted started it.

"It's lousy, nobody telling me. I go to war, get in a fight, lose two teeth. I come home, Al's after me—clean the tub, don't miss Mass. Can't we get going?"

"My car needs to warm up. The tires are still square. Don't be mad we didn't say anything to you about your dad, Pete. We knew he was in bad health. Give the car a minute. There, now we're set."

"Can't you floor it? You'd think my ma would've let me know if he was that bad. Maybe it's only a cold he's got. That's it. I can still leave town, drive down the alley, head south tomorrow. When I get to Iowa, I turn west to Camp Pendleton."

"You haven't driven your car two feet," Gunski said.

"When we get to Al's, pull around so I can check the

extension cord. Can't you go faster than twenty? I gotta get home to pack. It's a long trip to the West Coast."

Mrs. Dziedzic wouldn't stop crying when he walked in.

"I heard about him," Pete said.

"He got worse when I telephoned that you're talking about reenlisting. He won't go on long. I'll have to look after your dad when he can't walk to the mill."

She'd taken out her rosary.

"It's like we're no relation," Pete said. "He wouldn't tell me about the illness. I'm twenty-two years old, a war veteran gone four years. He was at work or the Polish lodge when I was growing up. I never knew the guy."

"He wanted to take you to the lodge, too," she was saying. "You were busy with your friends. Why don't you write him a note in the ovals of the Palmer Method I've taught you? Say, 'I'm sorry.' Say, 'I'm going to help, Dad. You, me … we'll get through it together.' Say the rosary with me."

"Where's my shaving kit?"

"At least leave him a note," she said. The beads clicked as she crossed herself with the rosary. "It'll provide him a sign of love. Tell him you joined the Kosciuszko Club. Tell him you're not reenlisting. You're staying home."

"I'm not kidding, Ma. Where's the shaving kit? I don't want you criticizing my handwriting if I write him. He never wanted me or my car here, like parking it by the garage will kill the dead winter grass."

"It's terribly cold. Your father's walked home in this kind of weather all his life. He goes to work in blizzards and cold."

"I'll write 'Sorry you're sick.' I've gotta prepare for my trip. When it comes to the Rambler, I don't want trouble. Tell Al I couldn't wait up for him. I've done my part to repair things between us. Here's the note you wanted me to write to him."

"I'll call the flour mill. 'Give your boy the sign he needs,'

I'll say. All these days and years I've said rosaries. Now he's dying, my husband's dying. *Jezu kochanej.*"

Pete could hear her sobbing on the telephone. "He's going to leave for Camp Pendleton. Now you do something to show *him* you love him."

Mrs. Dziedzic could hear Pete, too. Upstairs, the dresser drawer slammed, a wire hanger bounced on the floor.

Looking at the cloudless, starlit sky, Pete remembered that on such nights radiational cooling occurs when warm air escapes the earth. He didn't know why he'd remember this of all things. The bottom of the window had frost on it. Reflected in the pane above, he could see himself in the uniform he'd put on. He'd been awarded the Vietnamese Campaign Ribbon, Armed Forces Expeditionary Ribbon, National Defense Ribbon, Good Conduct Ribbon, and a Sharpshooter's Medal for qualifying on the rifle range. Through the window, he could see someone a half-mile away, his journey lighted by the moon in the clear sky.

Beyond Pete's mirrored face, beyond it and the Rambler that would start with the good tank heater, beyond the hill on the other side of the ravine where alder brush rises out of snow that contributes to radiational cooling, from out there in the moonlit night, here came the foolish old millhand. He'd walked off the job to see the son he'd been battling since the kid was a baby. The entire walk home, Al was muttering how the kid was ungrateful, how he might as well leave town, let Al die in peace and the war between them end. But there was this, too: Al recalling how he and Wanda had prayed that their son would be safe in Vietnam when he'd gotten his orders.

As Pete looked out the window, wondering what he'd done to deserve such a father, it seemed to him that Al was frozen in time, but he couldn't be, for he didn't have a moment to spare on this night. He'd passed beneath the Second Street viaduct. On the tracks down there was a laborer, a working stiff, on the way home from a lifetime at the flour mill.

For a minute, he lost sight of the old man as Al, deep in thought, walked down the alley and passed behind the garage. How many times Al had yelled at Pete—and the boy at the old man. There'd never be a sign of love and acceptance from Al Dziedzic, Pete realized when he lost sight of his father. There never had been a sign. If it wasn't the bathtub, it was something else. Thankfully, with the Rambler he had a way to escape. He'd never return. He'd reenlist for six years, then six more. When he got out, he'd be a master gunnery sergeant, a lifer. Who cared about anything back here in Superior?

"He's coming, Pete. Dad's on his way to your rescue. He'll save our family," Wanda called from the downstairs hallway.

Then there he was again, good old Al, the laborer, back in view the way he'd been in and out of view all of Pete's life. Wanda was right. There was the former Tuesday night bowler, the former railroad hand. As sick as he was, he'd made it from the mill to the car in the backyard. Now Al was circling the Rambler, peering in its windows, shaking his head. Pete couldn't figure out what Al was doing stooping down, as though he intended to pray. Maybe he's gonna pray for himself to make things right before God, Pete thought. Maybe I can pray and ask forgiveness on him.

Then he watched Al unplug the extension cord and with it the heat and power to the car battery. It looked as though he might be doing something with the tires. Pete observed the whole thing. Outside on this bitter night, unaware anyone was watching, the old man had found the strength to bend down and—and what?

The car would freeze up in an hour, maybe less. The Rambler was going nowhere, especially if it snowed, which would eventually happen. Whether in uniform or not, Pete wasn't going anyplace either, unless it was to Hudy's or the Warsaw Tavern. If Mrs. Dziedzic said enough rosaries, there was a slight chance the war could end, but probably not. In this cruel, desperate way, with the car's engine frozen, an old man would keep his young son here until they both died of the wounds that had been inflicted over the past twenty years.

"*Łatwiej przebaczyć, niż zapomnieć* ... It's easier to forgive than forget." That is what you could say about all of this. Or maybe, "*Jesien nie zrodzi czego wiosna nie zasiała* ... Fall will not grow what spring has not sowed." Though there's much else you could include about the love between father and son, that is about all you *really* could say here in Superior, Wisconsin, concerning the laborer and his lost son, Pete Dziedzic, who'd been to war.

The Shadow Players

Pete Dziedzic's teeth lay buried a half-mile south of the Da Nang Air Base. There the lance corporal had quarreled with a private over "Sea of Love." Guys in the outfit were singing along to Armed Forces Radio when Pete had said, "That singer's from the north."

"He's from Lake Charles," replied the private.

"No, he ain't," Pete said.

"Everybody's proud of him in my hometown. His name is John Phillip Baptiste, though on the record he changed it to Phil Phillips with The Twilights."

"You're wrong."

"You're wrong," said Private Abadee, hitting Pete so hard he swallowed one tooth and felt another dangling by a bloody thread.

"Hit him back," yelled the guys, but the lance corporal only asked for a towel to spit blood into. He was on "Queer Street." Rocked by a punch, prizefighters dwell here when they hang on the ring ropes trying to remember who they are. Staring at his flak jacket and M-14 on the wooden floor of the strong back tent, he took a laminated holy card with the Virgin's picture from his wallet. "Hail Mary," he said through his bloody lips as the guys sang along with the vocalist from Lake Charles, "I want to show you, h-o-o-w much I love you."

The next morning, Lieutenant Sardelli assigned a jeep driver to take Pete to the medical unit on the other side of Division Ridge. The driver wouldn't talk to a guy with no fight in him. Besides, the beauty of the limestone cliffs left them speechless, especially where tatters of silky mist hung from the quiet slopes. This was Vietnam: mists, black-pajamaed peasants planting rice, red laterite roads, monsoons, dry spells.

At the medical unit, helicopters swept in from a combat mission near An Ho. Men hollered, lifted stretchers, held IV bottles over wounded Marines. Nurses ran out to help them. It was no place for a person without courage.

In a part of the compound far from the landing zone, the Navy dentist looked up. Today's helicopter wounded wouldn't be worried about plaque buildup on their teeth, so Lance Corporal Dziedzic had saved the dentist from a boring day. Seating him in a chair, the dentist worked the tooth out of the lance corporal's mouth, packing the area with gauze to stop the bleeding. Eventually, the gums healed. Three weeks later, Pete, who'd prayed over and over to the holy card, opened the screen door and prepared to have a clay impression made of his upper gums.

In a few weeks, he had the new teeth. The partial plate hooked to the backs of his real teeth by means of curves in the bottom ridge of the plastic. The two false teeth fit into the slots left by the original teeth. Because the partial could be flipped in and out with the tongue, it was called a "flipper."

"Bite carefully. When you take it out, put it in a cup of water," said the dentist.

For a week, Pete was nervous about the partial. His hands had also shaken two months earlier. With everyone anticipating *El Cid*, the first movie during Pete's tour of duty, a jittery Marine, thinking he'd heard movement on the camp perimeter, shot up the darkness with a machine gun. This was the big one, Pete had thought as guys scrambled for helmets, flak jackets, rifles. As it turned out, the company wasn't being overrun. Ending up on Queer Street and losing two teeth was as bad as it got for the young man who'd rise to the rank of corporal before coming home, honorably discharged, to argue with his father toward the end of December.

What had happened to his teeth puzzled him when he

finally made it home from the war zone. The lieutenant had wrapped one in tissue paper and, putting up a hook shot, tossed it into the waste basket. Pete remembered a tooth resembling a lover's teardrop. Because he'd swallowed the other tooth when Private Abadee had hit him, that one must have been voided into the outhouse, the four-holer at the compound. Periodically, lime was poured over the contents and the outhouse returned to use. Seven or eight months later, the slanted roof, weathered boards, crude screen door, and plywood seat were doused with kerosene, burned, then covered with dirt and a sign put up: Head Closed.

One discarded in the garbage, the other buried in the dirt beneath the outhouse, the teeth were a part of the history of war. If buried teeth do not decompose, they are resting in the tropical earth beside a scrap of screen and a metal bracket from a charred outhouse door. Someone who had all his teeth and who'd not been to war might have wondered about other things during those days—who, for example, had ended up with his Joan Baez albums or at what time his fellow protesters were meeting for a drink at The Ramble Inn. In addition to the piasters Pete had spent drinking in the Da Nang Hotel on the afternoons he'd had liberty during that war year, he'd left two teeth in a country 65,948 square miles large.

In the friendly territory of the East End of Superior, Wisconsin (approximately two square miles), he'd lost even more. First, his girlfriend had slipped away from him. Then his father began leaving without Pete's discussing important matters with him. The girlfriend's departure was tough, but his being on active duty for four years had gotten to her. One night, she'd met a guy at The Purple Onion. "He looks like you, Petey," she'd told him when they bumped into each other outside of the East End Drugstore. Pete thought she was as pretty as ever. He wished they were back in time four years.

"I'm home. Now what am I supposed to do with my life?"

he asked. "I haven't seen you in a year."

"Dale works at Water, Light, and Power. Have you learned to drive? Have you got hair on your chest yet? You were twenty-one the last time we met."

"I bought a car. I parked it in the snow beside the garage. I take the driver's test tomorrow. It's my second try. No wonder my old man calls me '*Glupiec*, Blockhead.'"

"Good luck. Sometimes you fail the driving test. You'll make it this time."

"I better be able to drive. Dad is sick. He can't go anywhere. I have to do things for Ma."

"Your poor father."

"I'm back in my old bed. My sister teaches grade school in Shawano, doesn't get home much. I see the guys for a beer. What else is new?"

"Don't blame me for marrying. You weren't here. It was too long to wait."

"You're hitched. That's what I heard. I was gone in Vietnam. I like your parents."

"I like yours. Never blame your dad for anything in life, Pete. Say hi to your mother for me, and to him."

"He's next to go. It's funny. He was always on me. 'Cut your hair. Help with the dishes. Do this! Do that!' I feel terrible for fighting with him. Why'd we always argue?"

"Can't you ask him?"

"It's too late. The doc says he's dying."

Fortunately, Al stayed alive long enough for his son to talk about shadows. After Al drank a small cupful of morphine, when the old man was woozy but free of pain, Pete would begin the game. Morning sunshine on beige wallpaper is perfect for making silhouettes with your hands and fingers. "What do you see, Pa?"

"A camel's head," Al responded.

"No, a serpent. Try this."

"A duck."

"Good one. And this?"

"A cat."

"Excellent."

"I want to rest now," Al would say after a moment and turn his head from the wall. Seeing two-days' growth of whiskers on his father's thin face, observing Al's fingers twitching from the morphine as though practicing the silhouettes he'd later stump his son with, Pete would get up from his chair. "I'm going out," he'd tell his mother who busied herself in the kitchen.

Where they lived, February is the sunniest winter month. At eleven in the morning if you want to clear your head of the shadows your father has made for you, you can walk down Fourth, Fifth, or other East End streets that parallel the bay in Superior, Wisconsin. Confine the walk to between Twenty-Fourth and Twenty-Sixth Avenues, and you'll see elms, cottonwoods, willows, red osier dogwood, and alder brush casting shadows along the snowy hillside above the creek. The interweaving shadows of the cloudless days appear to long for someone. For what reason do the shadows of Superior, Wisconsin—or the mists of the Annamite Mountains of Vietnam—exist except to remind a marine and his Vietnamese counterpart that the shadows and the mists were there when they were boys?

In Al's shadowy room, the February light grew dim when the sun passed west beyond the window. Except during the shadow game, Al didn't talk. "Check his wristwatch, Pete. See is it keeping time for him." "Yes, Ma. We're still okay on the time," Pete said. Wanda brought her husband a can of protein drink for supper, solid food being difficult for him to swallow. One day a priest brought Al supper. Stomping his overshoes on the back porch before entering the kitchen, he said, "Peace to this house." "And to all who dwell therein," Wanda replied as Father sprinkled her with holy water and caught Pete with a sprinkle as he walked in.

Wanda had covered a TV tray with a lace doily. Next to the can of protein drink Al would have for supper, Pete had placed, in the form of a cross, two sticks of red osier dogwood. This scarlet bush grows all over the fields and woods around Superior. He thought his dad might be receiving what is called the "Viaticum" (the Holy Eucharist given to a dying person) in the form of the protein drink—which explains the wood cross: Pete hoped the cross sanctified his father's supper. In addition to evergreens and the moss that grows dark green in winter, the branches of the red osier dogwood give color to a snowy country.

If a dying person, whose pale skin resembles snow, is not up to it, the Church allows someone to say the "Confiteor" "in his name." This Wanda did for Al, whispering, "I confess to Almighty God, to Blessed Mary, ever Virgin, to Blessed Michael the Archangel, to Blessed John the Baptist, to the Holy Apostles Peter and Paul ..." Then Al drank the can of Ensure the priest handed him.

Father Mike enjoyed a can once he had ministered to the retired millhand. "Refreshing," he said. Having praised God for His plentiful gifts, including protein drinks, the youthful priest promised to return in a day.

When he left, Al reached for his teeth. As if uncertain whether he was still on earth, perhaps in Vietnam where his boy had been, he moved one hand tentatively, dreamily, over the blanket, then over the tray, looking for the teeth, but Al's uppers rested in a cup of water in the top drawer of the bedside table.

"You put them in for him, Pete."

"No, you put them in, Ma."

"Please, son, you have teeth missing. You know how to do it," she said. Wanda was crying.

Though Al lay in shadow, his son, wanting him to look good in heaven and realizing there'd be no talking about the past now, no apologizing for anything Pete had said or done to him, gently opened his father's mouth and put in the teeth. The mind is funny. Though this was no place for it, Pete found himself thinking about his own lost teeth.

There is an icon that is holy to Polish people. In Buffalo, New York, and Scranton-Wilkes-Barre, in Cleveland, Hamtramck, Chicago, Superior, the Poles keep Her image in their homes. They do this in Kraków, Łomza, Warsaw, Katowice. The Madonna in the icon wears a golden crown. Angels hover about it as they do on either side of the bejeweled crown of the child the Madonna holds in Her arms. Two scars disfigure Her right cheek. The scars, wounds that have saved the Polish nation over and over, were the work of seventeenth-century Swedish invaders who, after slashing Her beautiful face in a monastery, witnessed the icon's face bleeding and crying. Falling to their knees stunned, the Swedes retreated from the monastery at Jasna Góra, and Poland was saved. The Madonna's picture at Al and Wanda's had been reproduced on quarter-inch-thick wood, seven inches wide, ten long. A paper label on the back read "Made in Poland."

"Are you in pain again, dear Al?" Wanda asked her husband. "Drink this."

When he saw his father disoriented from the medicine, Pete lit the holy candles by the bed. He would practice his silhouette-making against the holy candles' light.

His face washed, teeth in, Al, having drunk the morphine, said, "Let me play for real tonight. That's a dog in the shadows on the wall."

"Yes, it's a dog," Pete said. "Does this look like an alligator?"

"Alley-gator," the old man said. "I hear someone crying."

Pete reshaped his fingers.

"A house, Father? A house like ours?"

"Cat."

"Right again."

"What's that on the ceiling?" asked Al.

"It's just evening," said Wanda. "The morphine makes you imagine things. You thought it was a butterfly. No one's crying."

This time Pete went out on a limb to trick him. He formed his hands and fingers this way and that. A crown in a flicker of candlelight is not easy to make. Nor is the Christ-child. Nor are a mother's scars. The morphine easing Al's pain, he lay watching. The room was silent as it should be when Jesus and Mary enter.

"What are you trying for now?" asked Wanda. Outside, the early-rising moon had brought shadows back to the hillside. "What is so hard for you tonight, Pete, like you are a craftsman in the old country?"

"I'm trying to solve shadow problems."

In the basement the furnace came on. The warm air blowing through the vent shifted the holy candles' light so that Pete had had to readjust his hands and fingers. "It's the draft doing this," he said. Try as he might, it was impossible in the shifting light to show them what he wanted—the Polish flags, the white eagle symbolizing that nation, the words "*Pod Twoją Obronę Uciekamy Się*" that translated mean, "To Your Protection We Flee." All of these things are on the icon of the Blessed Mary and Her Son.

"I think Dad knows what I'm trying to make," Pete said. "How do you know it though, Al? Tell us, when it's the first time I've tried forming this outline on the wall. Do you see it too, Ma?"

"Is it St. Adalbert? Is it St. Jadwiga?"

"No. Try someone else."

"Is it the dome of the Basilica of St. Josaphat in Milwaukee?"

"No, Ma."

"Is it a glider airplane? Is it a Polish soldier charging a tank?"

"Try harder. Look at the wall. Can't you see it in the outline?"

Making the sign of the cross, she knelt by Al's side, whispering the Polish words Pete was trying to read from the icon: "To Your Protection We Flee."

Given the seriousness of his condition, Al Dziedzic had not been restricted as to how much pain killer he could have. His hands rose into the air as if he were holding a chalice of wine, a wafer, a cup of morphine. In the half-light, his hands ran gently over something only he saw. Maybe a veil. Maybe a scar.

Trying to steady them, Pete took his father's rough hands.

"Why are you crying?" Al asked his wife and son. "Is it for me?"

"Who is? Who do you see? Is She in here crying?" Wanda asked.

"He's okay. He's doped up, Ma."

Pete ran his fingers over hands that had swung sledge hammers, hefted railroad ties, run conduit beneath a flour mill floor, accepted the Eucharist at Mass. The son's hands weren't tough from work. In the past months, he'd done little more than make outlines on a wall. He was nothing like his father.

He guided Al's hands down, knelt beside him. With his own hands calming his father's, Pete couldn't make the Virgin Mary's silhouette. He hadn't practiced enough. But this was only a silhouette, after all, and insubstantial. It didn't matter that Pete couldn't make it. Because when Al said something in Polish that sounded like "Holy Mother," Pete knew, as did Mrs. Dziedzic, Who had entered the shadows of the bedroom to match his father's suffering with Her own.

THE BIRD THAT SINGS IN THE BAMBOO

Thaddeus Milzewski was another one from Superior who'd been to Vietnam, twice in fact. The accident that earned him the Purple Heart could have been avoided if Sergeant Farrazzi hadn't been in a such hurry to get the food out to the grunts. As a result, the chow hadn't been secured when the truck left Da Nang. When the deuce-and-a-half veered sideways on a dusty road, twelve loaves of rye bread had pummeled the lance corporal's head and, with the lance corporal riding in back, a nine-pound ham had broken his ribs. He'd lost consciousness in a sea of chipped beef.

After a second harrowing tour in Vietnam, he'd cry out during the nights when he got home. "Where am I?"

His mother would rush in. "You're back. Your war days are over, son. You were calling, 'Help! Help!' Go to sleep. You've got college classes tomorrow."

"I can't sleep."

As he lay awake, he recalled how a simple thing like stirring cream corn and baking casseroles for the hungry troops had led to his present predicament. Instead of being stuck in the bush with an artillery or an infantry company during his second tour, he'd been free, for several hours each week, to go to the beach a few miles away to swim, drink beer, toss a football, or stare at the glistening sea—or at the young woman he couldn't forget.

She was sixteen, half-French, half-Vietnamese. He dreamed of her beautiful face, her finely formed hands and wrists, as early morning breezes rustled the elm trees outside the window of his boyhood home. When he first saw her, she'd been wearing a black silk shirt and pants. The flip-flops on her feet were made from recycled tires.

"You buy?" she'd said that day as he headed to the truck that would take him back to his outfit. "For you and frien' back at camp."

In a tray hanging from the rope about her shoulders were cigarettes and chewing gum.

"I'm Lance Corporal Milszewski of 'America's Dairyland' in Wisconsin. Pronounce my name right, and I'll buy from you," he'd said. "I've been here eight months. I'm on my second tour."

"Ta-doos," she'd said.

"No. 'Ta-*de*-oosh' is my first name."

Then she told him her name.

It sounded like "Quinn" or "Queen Vo" to him. He asked her to tell him the Vietnamese words for "beach," for "sand," for "the bird that sings in the bamboo." When he bought a pack of chewing gum and whistled to imitate the bird, she knew he meant *Son ca*. "Ve'namese farmer like that bird. Sing morning to night. It called 'skylark bird,'" she said. "When I try to learn English, soldier tell me what bird's name is in America."

What could he imitate for her next—water lapping against the fishing junk offshore, red eyes painted on its bow to ward off evil spirits? He told her he'd return on the next clear day for more gum.

"Khuyen Vo here in afternoon," she said. "Mother have shop where you can find me. She sells many things, but I carry only a little tray."

"We're allowed five hours here. I've got to go," he said, imitating the bird's song as he waved to her from up the beach.

That night with the guys talking and playing cards, he rearranged his belongings in a sea bag, wrote a letter to his parents. Later, in his cot beneath the mosquito net, he thought of

Khuyen Vo. At 0100 hours, 1 A.M., he imitated the skylark beneath his breath. The next morning when he stopped for a drink of water from the lister bag, he imitated the skylark, softly, and the morning after as he prepared French toast for the troops.

IN TWO WEEKS, HE RETURNED to China Beach. At the shops built of flattened cans and scrap wood, marines hung around drinking beer, Vietnamese rum, Coca-Cola. "Tiger"-brand cigarettes cost ten *piasters* a pack. But where was Khuyen Vo? He'd learned during his first tour not to pin his hopes on anything in this god-forsaken place. Still, when a voice said, "No buy cigarette?" he was afraid to turn around for fear it wasn't her.

"I never smoke, but I'll buy some gum," he said.

"What's my name?" she asked, smiling beneath the shade of her straw *nón lá* as she straightened it. She adjusted the rope on her shoulders that supported the tray.

"Queen," he said. "Here, let's split a stick of Doublemint. I haven't been here for a few weeks. I couldn't get away."

"I no stop work ri'now. Have to earn money."

"Just rest here," he said.

"I sit five minute, rest. Practice English."

The colored gum wrappers reminded him of the counter Mrs. Magnuson tended by the cash register in the East End drugstore back home. "Double your pleasure, double your fun," he said, unwrapping a stick of gum for her.

"I no often meet soldier like you," she said. "Only hear soldier gun shooting far away at night."

"They're firefights," said the lance corporal. "I'll protect you."

"How you protec'? You have sore leg. Can't go far. I watch you walk. You long time in Ve'nam? Have girlfriend? Why you sad when you talk to me?" she asked, savoring the taste of the gum.

"I was in an accident on my last tour here. No, I'm sure not sad, and no one's waiting for me at home. Do you have a boyfriend?"

"Khuyen Vo no have time for boyfrien' 'til she twenty-five. I someday go to Saigon Medical School. In two year' I want to take first 'concourse' exam to be a doctor. I go to school mornings."

When she smiled, he saw how white her teeth were. She'd reddened her lips. It looked as though she'd brushed them against a tropical flower. Her white teeth, olive-colored skin, black hair and eyebrows under the *nón lá*; he couldn't stop looking at her. The two of them sampled a piece of Spearmint next. "I promised I'd be here," he said. "How do you like this flavor?"

"Khuyen Vo like it because you buy from her," she said.

"In America you chew a flavor until you tire of it, then you switch. It's the same with many things," he said. "Your tray is like at the drugstore in the neighborhood where I live—except there you have twenty brands of cigarettes plus pipe tobacco plus cigars. Mrs. Magnuson sees that they're fresh or Art Haugen would get mad. He's the owner, but she's in charge of the greeting cards, newspapers, magazines, confections."

"I don't know what are those things," said Khuyen Vo.

"They're nice to have if you like variety."

"Ve'namese cannot double their pleasure very easy. That's why I want to go to Saigon, study. Then I help people. I study in school to learn English and science."

"So you have no boyfriend?"

"No interest. I tol' you I study and have no time. You don't listen."

She was right about him not listening.

After two more weeks, she was out of chewing gum. In the United States, twenty packs cost a dollar. Here he'd spent six dollars for twenty-one packs of gum and bought her out.

In addition to his pay, he was receiving an overseas allotment plus hazardous duty pay. What did he care what he spent?

"I like Black Jack, Dentyne, Beaman's Clove. There's a dance on TV advertising this one gum, Teaberry. You start with your legs together, then move them apart," he said. "The music for 'The Teaberry Shuffle' goes 'Ta-dadada-dada.' You skip your feet a little, scissor your legs fast, go back to— I look stupid imitating it for you, don't I? There's a railroad trestle by our house you get to by cutting through the woods where the smell in fall reminds you of Juicy Fruit. Aspen trees smell like that. Shutting my eyes, touching the cellophane on these cigarette packs, I can recall home like I'm there at the drugstore counter or fiddling with my buddy's pack of cigarettes. His car's running, I'm turning the radio dial, he's getting our food orders at the Frostop Drive-In. A lot of stuff brings you home in your mind so you're not in the war."

"Maybe in Saigon I will feel that way," Khuyen Vo said. "It far from family here. South Ve'nam government pay for the university and medical school. However, I must pass concourse examination to stay. When I leave here in two year, life is different for me in Saigon."

"I remember when I left home this last time. Man, I got drunk, worried, switched my thinking a hundred times about coming back to Vietnam, but now I'm happy I signed up for a second tour."

SHE RETURNED ONE DAY with a red flower from a *Phùòng* tree in town. As he practiced saying the name, she told him it symbolized the end of school since it always blooms in May. "To student who has vacation from school but will be separated from friend and teacher, the bloom of the *hoa Phùòng* represents sadness as well as happiness," she said. She was lucky to find the flowers so fresh because during the rainy season they fall from the tree.

In return for the flower, the lance corporal gave her a map. They unfolded it on a table behind her mother's shop. Khuyen Vo's mother didn't know whether to laugh or cry when she saw the Marine with her daughter. After introducing the lance corporal to *ma mére*, Khuyen Vo excused herself to listen to the American say, "This is the railroad trestle I told you about. These cross-hatched lines are like a symbol for it."

"What this?"

"Neighborhood school, not mine though. The river is the 'Nemadji.' It means 'Left-Handed River.' When Indians and French fur trappers came off of Lake Superior, they saw the river on the left."

"French people like in Ve'nam? They look like me?" she asked.

"Yes, French. They named places *Bois Brule, Au Sable, Isle Royale.*"

The topographical map showed low spots and elevations of hills, bays, rivers, creeks. Dots represented houses. Before he'd left home, he circled his own house in red. Parallel lines, a shovel, flags, and crosses indicated railroad tracks, a sandpit on Wisconsin Point, schools, churches. The long edge of the lake was blue.

They spent twenty minutes looking at the map. He handed her a stick of Juicy Fruit to give her an idea of the scent of his country in the fall. "Here's my grade school. These are neighborhood houses," he said. "There's St. Francis Church. It and mine, St. Adalbert's Church, are marked by a cross on top of the black square. I know it's hard to follow, but this is East Fourth Street. I walk it a lot going to and from the East End business district. Khuyen Vo, this is beside the point, but at the Superior Theater when I was in high school, there were talent contests. After the movie Friday night, local people like Mr. Buck Mrozek, who played 'The East End Polka' on the accordion, all competed. There were great bands playing. The winner was to appear on Jack Paar, this famous TV show. Besides

Buck Mrozek, now that I think of it, a few other old people had talent acts, but nobody except a band like 'Chet Orr and the Rumbles' had a chance because us teenagers always cheered for them. Week after week the competition went on. Just as the excitement peaked, the guy sponsoring the shebang took off. The police found out there'd been no arrangement made for anyone to be on Jack Paar."

"Where did he go?"

"Skipped town. Someday I could take you to the show house. I'd buy you a malt at the drugstore. We'd eat hamburgers at the Arrow Café."

"I want to attend medical school."

"Why not study in the U.S.? There's a hospital halfway between St. Adalbert's and my house. See it here where I was born? Maybe you could be a doctor in this hospital."

To help her daydream about the United States and about how near his parents' red-circled house stood to the river, she asked to keep the map.

"If you'd like to have it, that'd be great," he said. He told her Wisconsin got cold in winter. When the river froze, people skated on it. "One time my grandpa caught a sucker through the ice that was record size and written about in our newspaper."

"The Mekong is only river here with giant fish that can be ten feet long. I sometimes eat *pla bük*. Maybe you cook for me?"

"I do enough cooking at the mess tent," the lance corporal said.

"Then you cannot expect Khuyen Vo to cure you when you need a doctor," she said, teasing him.

HER WANTING THE MAP ... THE lance corporal's cornering the chewing gum market; how could this hurt anyone when he had five months left in Vietnam? When she brought more red flowers, he gave her a miniature magnifying glass so she could read the topography of his home more easily. During the rainy season, she turned seventeen.

A few days later she guided his hands to her face. She listened to his heartbeat. They met almost every day through the end of September. One day that month, as she taught him to shape the red flower into a butterfly, he kissed her eyes when she closed them, and the butterfly flower dropped to the earth. Another time, when they were alone in the palms and banana plants behind her mother's shop with only the sound of the bird in the bamboo, she told him that Saigon was four hundred and fifty miles through the highlands if she could travel the French Colonial highway. After she explained how she'd take another route because the old highway was dangerous, Khuyen Vo returned the lance corporal's kiss.

FROM THESE MATTERS OF butterfly flowers and interludes among the banana plants, Khuyen Vo's love grew for the lance corporal, and she remained happy and trusting. The lance corporal, however, suspected that in his own case either the East End winters or Vietnam's rainy weather had done something terrible to his heart.

It was the first of October. Coincidental with one of their afternoons together an opportunity came for him to return to the States early. Three hours after the lance corporal told Khuyen Vo he'd never leave her, Thaddeus's gunnery sergeant decided to delay his own rotation to the United States until later in winter. That way he could take his wife to the St. Paul Winter Carnival. Then he would settle in to await a beautiful spring in Quantico, Virginia, his next duty station. Fond of the lance corporal, especially of the way he prepared a Polish meal, the gunny said, "You take my rotation day, Milszewski. You have as much time in Vietnam as I do this tour. I'll give you an earlier travel slot. How's the beginning of January? I'll cut your orders if you want out of here. A good cook deserves the gratitude of his nation."

How often the lance corporal dreamed of home. Though it would be twelve below zero and snow would be piled high on the roadsides, he'd be in Superior much sooner than planned if he accepted the gunny's offer. Considering the possibilities life now presented, he'd propose marriage to Khuyen Vo the next time he saw her, and later, on China Beach, they'd figure out the details of their life together. If he wanted to rotate ahead of time, he'd still have a few months with her before having to make up his mind.

As they walked up the beach the next afternoon, he thought, Why worry her now? Why tell her I might leave? The day was too beautiful for anything so serious. She made him stay in the dune grass while she walked to the shore. "What are you doing?" he called to her.

"I show you where *I* live," she said.

With a stalk of sea grass, she drew lines in the elevation in the sand near where he sat. Where the slope in the sand was sharper, her contour lines ran closer together. On a topographical map, intervals between lines meant a ten-foot rise. After plotting the land, she drew an outline of his fingers, writing beside the outline the words she was whispering as she ran her other hand over the scar on his leg. She brought her face to his neck, lay against him so that they could watch the forest beyond the dunes.

He kissed her. (Why tell her anything right now? Why not surprise her once the gunny's news sank in? He could return home, go to college, send for her.) When he put his hands beneath her silk shirt and kissed her, she kissed him, too. When he told her he'd never leave someone so beautiful and that one day they'd be married, he wondered why she looked sad. "I won't ever leave you, you know that," he said. They lay in the sun protected from the sea breeze by the dunes. He told her there were places like this where he lived. He pretended now that they were in northern Wisconsin and she was going to meet his parents.

"Will your family be on the beach of Lake Superior?" she asked, going along with his game.

"Yes, that's their driftwood fire down closer to the light-house."

"Will they like to meet Khuyen Vo?"

"They know you from my letters."

"Will you be happy?"

"Sure. I'll take you all over town. Dad's a regular fellow. When you see it, you'll like my room at home. My sister had polio when we were kids, but she had an operation. She's okay. Ma's nice. My best friends are Bob Harnisch and Norm Lier. I have plenty of friends. Wait'll you see the neighborhood—" He couldn't stop talking.

"So they like me?"

"Yes," he said, sad to pretend, but not wanting to betray any more than he had to about his plans. It was best not thinking about anything but who might see them when they wanted to be alone. "Wait," he said as she undid the front of her black silk shirt. Certain no one was in sight, he reached for her and helped her off with her clothes.

"You're not sure you want to go home, are you, Milszewski? I don't want to force it on you," Gunnery Sergeant Fiandt said one day. "You got a girlfriend, I hear. Don't even think about bringing her Stateside. It'll never happen. Do you think our government gives a shit every time a twenty-year-old Polack jarhead with blue balls thinks he's in love? Shit, the red tape involved in such a marriage would drive a person buggy. Nobody's *that* much in love to bring a Vietnamese woman to the land of the brave and the free! If you passed all the paperwork through on our side, which you probably would never get done, then you'd still have the South Vietnamese government fucking you over. They surely will, Ski, if you try to get her out of the country. Just as ARVN soldiers ain't worth a shit, neither is their government."

"I might leave her here for awhile, Gunny. I'm not sure. I know it's a lot of red tape to get her out of Vietnam, but I've got to try," the lance corporal replied. "I'm looking forward to a good, long rest in Superior where I can think things out and decide."

"You deserve a rest," said the gunny. "Get your head screwed on, Ski. You don't need something like this mucking up your life. You don't want a slant-eye who prob'ly can't talk English walkin' down the aisle on your wedding day. No, do as your gunny advises. Keep your other head in your pants, and you'll be fine. Pray or something when you're together with her. It's only a temporary urge you feel for her. Hell, Ski, go to 'Dog Patch' if you need to get laid. You'll get your ashes hauled for three-hundred *piasters* and not have the red tape to worry about afterwards."

"I'll think about 'Dog Patch', Gunny, and about everything you say. I know things work against a person in life sometimes, so it's good to think things through."

"That's the ticket, Ski, to have plans."

STILL, THERE WAS THIS GIRL. At 2 A.M.—0200 hours—listening to small arms fire far away, he knew what his options were: either stay in Vietnam or go back home and find someone new in the States. Fifteen times he began letters home. "I'm staying here. I found somebody I love," he'd write his parents. Then he decided he'd return to Wisconsin and tell his congressman that she needed medical assistance, that they were married, that the government had an obligation to him, Tad Milszewski, citizen, veteran, to get her out of Vietnam. He told himself so many things he tired of thinking about them.

Then it was 5 A.M. Worn out with indecision and lack of sleep, he stacked eggs beside the stove and tinkered with the knob on the toaster.

WHEN THE SEA GREW ROILED and clouds shrouded the Anna-mites, he gave her a Marine Corps ring he'd bought at the PX in Da Nang. "Wear it on a string around your neck, Khuyen Vo. We're engaged," he said. He gave her his old transistor radio. She was pleased with the thoughtfulness of a marine who, though she didn't know it, had gotten himself into some-thing very deep. *Nobody* spent three tours in Vietnam! If he signed on for another one, his buddies in the outfit and people back home would think he was crazy. When he gave her the ring, he placed his hand on the map in a kind of pledge to her. "Remember, you're visiting home when you look at the map. You won't want to leave East End," he told her. They whispered their love to each other for so long a time that day that he'd had to run to catch the liberty truck.

That evening she held the map and the ring and tried to play his transistor, but her lover had forgotten to change the batteries. Flushed with the excitement of their lovemaking, the lance corporal didn't think about rotating until the hour before midnight.

An eagle, globe, and anchor decorated the gilded sides of the ring. The clerk at the PX had told him the smooth red stone in the center was a "garnet," the birthstone for January. After a week, Khuyen Vo was wearing the ring on her finger.

"Here's a photograph of our house," he told her when they met again in early January. "My parents' room is upstairs. It's behind these two windows. My room and my sister Anna's room are upstairs on the opposite side of the house. We can see Lake Superior from most every room in the house. You can keep the snapshot. To have a picture of the house will add to the meaning of the map for you."

"What room is ours?" asked Khuyen Vo.

"I guess my room will be ours. I'll get a job at the Water and Light as the night janitor. I know I can do it. We'll stay with my folks for a few months. Eventually, we'll need our own place. An apartment at the Euclid Hotel should be nice."

To steel himself as he described their future, he pulled out a newspaper movie ad from his wallet. He'd kept the ad since he left home. It read, "HUD—'The Man with the Barbed-Wire Soul.'" "Best movie ever," he told Khuyen Vo. Though the lance corporal didn't have a barbed-wire soul, he felt like he did as he tried to think how he could reconcile his desire for Khuyen Vo with the gunny's advice. Maybe the best thing would be to think of Paul Newman in "Hud." Hud had women around, but he stayed cool. He never fell for them.

Khuyen Vo was so beautiful. "Do you love me, Ta-doos?" she asked him.

"I love you more than anyone. I'll take care of you," he said.

As they walked along the contoured shore, she asked what it meant to have a soul of barbed wire.

"It's a way of saying you have no feelings. When I close my eyes—I have to shut them real tight and clear my mind—then I can't feel."

"You stay here with me?"

"I will. I was thinking if I ever went Stateside, it'd be only until I could make some plans for us."

"You're not going. Now is January. You stay, Ta-doos, 'til May and June like you tol' me?" she said, sensing his indecision.

"I'm not leaving," he said. "We're getting married in spring, I guarantee. But I might have to go home to prepare things for us."

Hearing this, she started crying, though the lance corporal couldn't understand why since he felt good about the future. She wouldn't stop crying until he reassured her. As he did, he tried to clear his mind to get back to what the gunny said.

"Why your eyes closed, Ta-doos?" she asked.

IN VIETNAM, ROADS OF RED LATERITE soil become greasy mud in the rain, a few pieces of fish mixed with rice and some greens provide a family three or four satisfying meals, and Khuyen Vo's mother chewed betel nut, which contained a mild narcotic to numb the pain in her gums.

The lance corporal remembered all this a week later as the C-130 flew over China Beach to Kadena Air Force Base in Okinawa. From there, he flew fourteen hours more to Marine Air Station, El Toro, California, for debriefing and discharge. Two days later, he flew on Western Airlines to Minneapolis, then on Republic Airlines one-and-a-half-hours to Duluth.

In Superior, the lance corporal, who'd taken the gunny's advice and not said good bye to Khuyen Vo, slept away the mornings in his parents' house. Why get worked up? He'd have had to rotate sooner or later, he told himself. For an enlisted man to bring a Vietnamese woman to America was nearly impossible; the gunny's words were ringing in his ears.

But by napping during the day, he couldn't sleep at night. Sometimes he remembered who had the topographic map. When his heart raced and there was no one but himself to listen to it, he thought of the bird that sings in the bamboo. In his boyhood bedroom, the one Khuyen Vo couldn't see in the picture, he thought of her and heard crows squawking outside chiding him for being like Hud. In an effort to free his soul from the coil of wire, he went to confession. "I did something to a woman," he told the priest on the Feast of St. Blaise in February. When the priest, who disliked the war, asked, "What, Thaddeus?", the penitent said he'd fooled a woman into thinking they were getting married. "It was the only way to keep myself sane," Thaddeus said. "You'll have to make it right with her," said the priest. But when Father asked where the woman lived, and Thaddeus, seeking absolution in a confessional booth in the East End, told him, "Da Nang, South Vietnam," the priest realized all was hopeless. "There's no penance I can give you for that," he said and closed the confessional screen on him.

PERHAPS IT WAS ON THE afternoon of this confession that the delicate Khuyen Vo believed her Marine would bring her more engagement presents. She twisted the garnet ring from side to side trying to read her future in the red stone. When February passed and the American with his wedding plans didn't show up, she sang the mournful song of a woman who waits for her lover by the Perfumed River. Her mother hummed along. In the shop hung a picture of a bridge beside which *Phùòng* trees bloomed. "Someday flowers will bloom in our houses," she told her mother, sighing as she watched the rain make the roads impassable. In Vietnamese, she whispered to herself, "I am waiting a long, long time." When the rain stopped, she re-plotted the distance from the sea to the dunes. "Ta-doos," she said, drew lines in the sand with her fingers, then said the name again.

By May when certain red flowers almost the color of garnet bloom on trees in the schoolyards and along the banks of the Da Nang River, Khuyen Vo, still pining for Thaddeus Milszewski, gave the American's map to an ARVN soldier who hung it in a jungle post hidden behind a fortress of orchids. In a few months, the Viet Cong overran the post, as they would eventually overrun the country. Puzzling over the intelligence value of the map, the VC looked for hours at the "NE/4 Superior 15' Quadrangle of Superior, Wisconsin." Especially disconcerting to them was a red-circled dot. What did it mean to their war effort, Milszewski's house by the river in Superior?

Meanwhile, the lance corporal was beginning to feel like his old self. He attended Mass, looked up friends. He couldn't believe he'd thought of staying in Vietnam. He was happily working part-time at the Water and Light. The autumn turned out to be beautiful. The yellowing aspen trees, the reddening maples brought out the leaf watchers in record numbers. Late into September, newspapers ran front-page photographs of the brilliant foliage along the Left-Handed River, and people swam in the lake. Before work on the evening of his birthday in mid-October, Thaddeus Milszewski could see from his window driftwood fires up and down the beach.

On the G.I. Bill, he had enrolled in the state teacher's college in Superior. He was progressing very well in school, especially in geology class. While the younger students complained of having to memorize the texture of minerals, he learned, to his pleasure, that the course also concerned beaches and the reading of maps. When these topics came up in October, he was ahead of his classmates, for he knew topography and felt his barbed wire soul to be completely healed from the maps of the past. But now he learned something new about map-reading: That you could place aerial photographs side by side, then view them from a few inches above through magnified lenses. Stereoscopic viewing makes the subject of the photos appear three-dimensional. When he discovered that virtually all the world's beaches have been photographed, he put his heart to a test to determine whether it was truly healed. It was kind of a mid-term test of his emotions.

That afternoon in geology class, he failed the test, the midterm, when he observed China Beach made so realistic that his tears blurred the stereoscope's lenses. He also began whispering about the action of waves upon a beach. "The tide shaped everything the whole time I was with you, Khuyen Vo," he told the beautiful Vietnamese woman with the garnet ring. His classmates listened for a while. Then they looked at one another and began rolling their eyes. As others snickered about his confession, calling him "the War Hero" and "the Lover" then turned in their tests, the former lance corporal went back to his stereoscopic viewing. "I couldn't help what I did to you," he was saying to an empty classroom and to the lover he was looking for in the rain on the dunes.

The harder he focused his attention through the lenses, the more he imagined the grains of sand they'd let slip through their fingers as they spoke of love. After all these months, he imagined her with someone new, this time a Vietnamese soldier who'd honor beautiful Khuyen Vo despite the shifting tides of war.

That left the American with his stereoscopic views to try to forget what had happened, though he never would, for he also knew that she had studied openly and honestly the map of his heart, had longed for him and loved him, and that now she, Khuyen Vo, would have nothing more to regret. To the lance corporal, this was the worst part of the stereoscopic view. And the memory of the bird songs that kept returning. And the memory of the red flowers, the *hoa Phùòng*.

Rain, Fog, a Harbor City

On a map, the north and south shores of Lake Superior meet to form what resembles an arrow point. We live at the point of the arrow. This and many other arrows pierce us at the Head of the Lakes.

Here is a kind of word postcard. You can't buy such a postcard at the counter of Lignell's Drugs or the Globe News because I, Bobby Harris, have made it up. Imagine this on the postcard: Weeds that grow over rusted railroad tracks, no diesel locomotives slowing for railroad crossings, no ore boat whistles ever piercing the foggy noon. Berthed at the docks in town are these old ore carriers rusting in the rain. The tracks leading to the docks rust. Two or three boats have been torn apart for scrap. Plenty others await the cutting torch. Not ten feet from the back door of my old man's tavern, three big ore boats rise up out of murky water. During bad weather, they've broken loose and drifted across the bay. Another berth holds Inland Steel Company vessels; another berth, Cleveland Cliffs Co. vessels. Except for the rust and chipping paint, they're ready to carry iron ore from here to Ohio once the steel mills on the lower lakes start up again. This is Superior, a town where the only things left are the drinkers and drunks.

Please don't ask for my next two word postcards at Lignell's Drugs or the Chamber of Commerce office. One of the postcards I dream up will have a picture of the Northern Pacific dock in East End. To my old man, the dock is a palace of industry stained red with ore dust. Creosoted beams rise up, then give way to these concrete arches which support the tracks and the trains that used to run high up there when ore was shipped to East Chicago, Detroit, and Cleveland. Nothing goes on up there now.

The other postcard is of the bar. It's a word postcard signed by me, the artist. Outside hanging up over the door in the word postcard is a big neon heart of pink with a jagged break in it, my sign, and the words Heartbreak Hotel. In the tavern my dad owns, a glass of beer costs a quarter; a bowl of beer, fifty cents. Add thirty-five cents, and you get a shot of whiskey or brandy. Sometimes this is called a "bump 'n a beer" or a "one 'n one." Most know the combination as a "boilermaker." People in here use other terms: "shot glass," "bowl of beer," "bar tab," "bar rag," and one hundred words and phrases beginning with "bar" or "beer," like "bar salami" or "beer chaser." They tell each other how drunk they got. They yell at each other for falling off of bar stools.

These word postcards I've made up are a kind of insider's map of the town. Then there's the map of the inside of me, the map of my heart, which is a dark, spiritless series of hills because I know I'm never leaving here. This much I haven't made up: I'm Bobby Harris. High School grad. Brown Hair, Blue Eyes. Here is how a map of the heart works: My parents, now in their late fifties, had me later in life when Ma retired and it was more convenient for her to think about children. I love her in spite of the work she used to do. My old man's the one who causes the map to curl up at the edges of my heart. "You're always hangin' around the docks. What are you looking for?" he says. He owns a business but drinks up most of what he makes. We're so poor at the end of the month that my dad has to cheat the government out of surplus food commodities or the fuel-assistance money the county provides to needy families.

If you're poor like we are because of the old man and if you go once a month for free flour and cheese at the Community Services Agency, you'll see the drinkers lining up across the street for a drink or three to get the day started. My old man's seen it all—meanness, public sin, men and women violating everything. I've seen a lot, too. My heart is shattered neon. It should be put up outside Heartbreak Hotel to blink on and off in the fog. It's one hill after another for me. They're getting bigger. Now Ma is sick. She aches. "I'm too warm," she tells me when I come in one night and fold a sheet over her. "Now I'm chilled," she says. I put a blanket on her and get another one, all the time wondering where in the hell the old man is.

"Feeling better?" he says. It's 2:30 A.M. He didn't even know she was sick, and he comes in asking her this.

"Some better," she says.

"You don't look so good," he says.

"Can I make you a sandwich out of the cheese Dad cheats the government out of, Ma?" I ask.

"She ain't hungry. Neither are you," he says. He wants the cheese all for himself.

She has this corrosive effect on him. They get along, but there are times when he says he needs his freedom. On such nights, he sleeps on a cot in the bar. This evening, or morning, Ma is corroding his spirit. He's had too much Royal Bohemian beer. On the way home, he said he'd looked forward to seeing his Magda snoozing. He'd have kissed her, maybe cried a little, he told me. But here instead of a good sob over his old, broken-down wife, and over himself—what a hapless, drunken fool he's become—he's had to play nursemaid.

(Another word postcard: I hope the poor, dear people of this city breathe smoke and soot up to the last; that their cries for beer go strangled by foghorns that never stop; that ore trains, after the final run to the harbor, toss cinders at their dead eyes; and that, at some time, the whole place gives up and caves in like East Chicago, Gary, and Michigan City, Indiana. That's how I hate the smoke and soot. Then I'll turn off the sign of my heart and throw away the map.

But the hills get bigger. People in the bars know what I do. I wait outside for them to bring me beer. Then we drive to Connor's Point for a drink. Then, depending upon the stars and the moon—

Heartbreak Hotel would be obscured in my mind if it weren't for the sign going on and off. Bobby Harris. Bobby Harris. The biggest sign on the waterfront reads DANCING. At first, you don't see the building itself, but the red neon DANCING sign of Johnny's Tavern. Sometimes I go dancing there. The Whoop 'n Holler Tavern, on the other hand, has a revolving light on its roof. The light guides the drinkers and drunks, who also guide me from the dance floor. Abigail's Dirty Shame Saloon has other enticements. All that Heartbreak Hotel, my dad's place, has is a jukebox and the sign of a broken-down heart. You hear the music all up and down North 3rd, echoing over the water and off the bows of rusting boats just a broken heartbeat away.)

STAN HARRIS, THE OLD MAN, puts himself on automatic pilot every day of the year. It's remarkable to see him go through the fog to the bar—left on Banks Avenue, right on Baxter, foggy, two block jaunts down alleys, right on North 3rd. He comes rolling down the street with the fog. In the gray, curling mist, you can't hear a thing. There will be a gray jacket up ahead and a man inside saying "How are you?" Pierced by the arrow called "the Head of the Lakes," he's no more than an outline in the fog.

"What are you doing?" he asks Ma now at three A.M. on another night.

"I can't get rid of the spots on me," she says. When she rubs her fingers together, they turn red. He sees a fine dust on my mother. Her arms and neck have red marks. The marks, the lesions, under the face powder on her neck are an inch wide.

"They don't hurt," she says, "but they bother me. What do you suppose they are, Stan? Am I becoming a rose?"

She gets up for a bath. She's been attempting to cover the things on her arms.

"I brought some beer," he tells her. He turns down the pressure cooker in which I've been preparing the old man's late-night supper. Now I draw Ma's bath, fix her couch.

"What are these?" he whispers. They look like the petals of a corroded rose.

"Did they come off of her arms?" I ask.

He tosses them in a wastebasket. "I don't know," he says.

"Did you clean the bathtub, Magda?" he asks Ma when she's done in there. She doesn't answer. He tries again. "Did that *National Geographic* come in today's mail for the boy? Do you want a beer?"

"No, no, I'm tending to my roses," she says from the bedroom.

"So you're not thirsty for a beer? I'll have one myself then. And if you're gonna stay in the bedroom, I might as well damn shut off the humidifier in here"

He brings a beer to her room, setting it on the nightstand. "I guess I'll be off to bed myself. I cleaned my dishes," Pa says. He kisses her forehead. We notice the fine powder on the pillowcase around her head.

"You coming to sleep?" he asks me.

"Yeah."

The old man turns on the vaporizer. It sputters and puffs. The windows steam up.

"No," she says concerning the vaporizer as I leave her room.

Before sleep, I dream of roses. All of a sudden, they line the side of our house. They are a deep, rich red. Sometimes they nod in the fog.

Up here in Superior, which in the old man's mind stands at the angle in the letter "L" in the words WATER, LIGHT & POWER CO. at the gas plant; sometimes in this part of the world, northwest winds bring rain and fog that corrode everything, even the goodness of your heart. Both the lake and the town lie frozen solid the other months of the year. This is what happens during the five frozen months: Drinking becomes heavy, the drinkers become desperate, life hangs suspended in the ice, the foghorns don't blow, hearts tear and break away in the cold. Once in the dark months, a man propositioned me with a box of government cheese.

"It's all I've got. No money left, and I heard you were an understanding kid."

"No," I told him, "you've gotta at least give me enough for beer money."

I dream of never going again to Heartbreak Hotel. I dream of saving money and hitting the good bars of Superior. I'd go up the street and put my broken heart behind me. I'd dance at the Androy Hotel. A fast or slow dance, it wouldn't matter, whatever they wanted, just so someday I danced out of here on the arm of a stranger.

ALMOST EVERY DAY ON HIS WAY to work or somewhere, my old man passes the gas plant I mention above. There is this huge metal globe maybe eighty feet high for the storage of natural gas.

"It's like a little world," he always says. "Look up at it. There's the gas ball, the steel sides … then we got the bay and air and water. All of it, all the elements of life to make it worth living in Superior. Everything's right here."

Where the equator would be on a map, here's a seam bolted by rivets running around the gas-plant globe. SUPERIOR WATER, LIGHT & POWER CO. is painted in blue on the side. With the six-pack he's bought Ma in the crook of one arm, the old man points with his other hand. "Just look, that's the Great Lakes up there where it's painted blue," he says. "Look at Detroit and Cleveland. Detroit's right where the bottom of the 'G' starts to make its turn to go up. See the line of rust there? The only rust on the whole WATER & LIGHT globe is around the Great Lakes."

I think of how someday the legs supporting the globe will rust, the globe collapse, the whole city be gassed. I tell him this.

"Gassed or rusted," he says. He sits on the tracks, opens a beer.

It's the weather which causes unprotected things to fall apart. Moisture gets in the wood. In time, the wood rots and crumbles under the touch. Iron oxidizes. At first you can rub the rust off with your hand. But if you wait, it takes a wire brush and hard scrubbing to get it done. And some things are impossible to clean.

"IT'S RUST," THE DOCTOR SAYS, "honest-to-goodness rust." It's a week later. "Your wife is rusting to death, Mr. Harris. Do you understand?"

She is out of hearing in the next room at the clinic.

"Her blood has excess iron," the doctor says. "You don't normally get hemochromatosis if you aren't taking iron pills, and you've said she wasn't."

"No," Pa says.

"We're going to have to bleed her each week. Her skin's going to bronze. It'll only get worse. Her body's an old car."

"I believe it's the moist air," Pa says.

"It could be," says the doctor

We take her home. She's got gloves on. Around her poor, dear red neck, she has tied a scarf to keep moisture out. A foggy, wet afternoon in Superior, the sun has little chance of breaking through. It's close to three o'clock. We'll fix dinner, fill the vaporizer, put her to bed. No, no vaporizer ... but we'll make her comfortable in other ways. It'll be best to keep her dry.

The old man is confused. He needs a drink. He's shaking more and more. "What if it's contagious?" he says. "Ain't we seen rust laying waste to Duluth-Superior?"

He's right. It spreads from building to building, over rail-road tracks. It eats at ore boats behind Heartbreak Hotel. I think of an Edgar Allan Poe story we read in high school. Now it's like the Red Death has the right-of-way here, too.

Ma ain't happy. She makes coffee and sits at the table as he empties water from the vaporizer. "At least I know how I'll end up when my time comes," she says, "no more wondering."

"I'm drying every bit of water in the tub and sink. I'm wiping down the windows, Ma," I say. Then I turn on her TV shows.

"I'll be going out awhile. I've got a lot to think about, Mag," says the old man who can hardly control the shakes. He's got a woman at the bar. Younger than him, he calls her his "Dolly." This has been going on for ten years, him and women.

"I understand why you're going," she says.

"But I don't understand it, Ma. I know you're becoming a rose and shouldn't he stay home because of it? Shouldn't he? You're just a beautiful flower. Why does this happen?" I ask her. She's all by herself most evenings and vulnerable to atmospheric conditions.

THE FOG WILL HIT HIM for acting this way toward Ma. He'll feel it seeking places to enter his unbuttoned shirt cuffs. Hoping to carry less moist air into his lungs, he'll bundle his jacket about him and breathe through his nose. It's how he is. There's no money for hospitals or for bleedings in the doctor's office, so he'll stumble down the alley to Heartbreak Hotel, which won't make many things better. The old man's got iron in his heart, but it's different from Ma's. He won't rust. His heart will just get hard. And why is it, I wonder, that some are spared? In the bar, he'll make jokes concerning Ma. "Call the junkyard," he'll say, "see what price scrap metal's getting."

A PERILOUS FOG HAS COME between us all. I know of no place that isn't rusting. All her married life my mother has sat here watching TV and becoming proficient in the Art of Pressure Cooking. He never took her anywhere. And before that, when she was a working girl, she stayed in, too. Now her heart is oxidizing.

He calls, crying over the telephone. "I'm drinking. Lemme talk to Ma." I don't put her on. I know rust is attacking the hearts and homes of out-of-work men—in Detroit, Cleveland, Buffalo, in all the cities and towns where plants have shut down and where the dampness invites its way in. They have nowhere to go but the Whoop 'n Holler, Dew Drop Inn, and Boiler Room Tap.

It's from disuse. The men in Cleveland and Detroit are rusting from disuse and misuse. Now my own mother suffers this affliction. For years, the old man left her home when he'd go to work. Without purpose in life, she took no precautions against rust, just sat home applying moisture cream to her face, bathing whenever she chose, and using the vaporizer freely. Sometimes she'd leave water standing in dirty dishes. It was that, the hemochromatosis, and the disuse.

The next morning we see a used car dealer about rust protection. Not before the old man reads up on oxidation, however. Before he can sweep, mop, and empty ashtrays, the stools are occupied, so I have to help him.

"Bump and a beer?" he asks a customer.

Behind the bar, the pickled pig's feet nestle in a jar.

"Nah, only beer today. I'm a little hung over."

"Big head, Ern?" the old man asks another customer.

"Yeah."

"Bowl or glass, Gus?" All day long, it's the same.

"Bowl."

"Joe, what's for you this morning?"

"Maybe some Petri's will warm me up. What d'you think?"

"Here's to ya," the old man replies and rings it up.

That's where the picture is, "Le Tombeau des Lutteurs,"

hanging behind the cash register. The words "The Tomb of the Wrestlers" are printed at the bottom. It's copied from a real painting by this French guy of a room in somebody's house. You can't see much of the room, just some shadowy blue corners, because, of all things, what's growing right inside takes up all the space. What is it but a rose, a big rose whose petals are red, deep, and inviting? It just kind of overwhelms the room and the air in it. But I don't understand the title.

Ma's never taken iron pills, but iron is in her body. If she cuts herself, she'll bleed it. "'The rusting of iron,'" Pa reads from a book called *Elementary Metallurgy*. He reads so loud and hard the customers look up. "'Iron combines with oxygen and water ... forms hydrated iron oxide.' What does it all mean?" he asks. He goes on some more. "'The oxide is a solid which retains the same general form as the metal from which it was formed, but is porous and somewhat bulkier. Being soft and weak, it renders iron useless for structural purposes.'"

I start then. "'Fortunately for the peace of mind of the beginning rose grower, the rose is an exceptionally tough and normally healthy plant and is troubled by relatively few diseases or cankers.'" It's from *Roses for Every Garden*. The old man's watching. "'Diseases behave in a rather peculiar manner.' Listen now," I say. "'They may appear during one summer and not another, so the fact that a disease attacked this year does not necessarily mean it will come again to plague you next year.' See! Ain't it proof that Ma can get better?" I ask.

But as I discover how to care for roses, he discovers how to prevent rust: Iron can be alloyed, which makes it resist corrosion; it can be treated with a substance that would "react preferentially with air and water, and thus, while being consumed, protect the iron," says his book. Or, he goes on, iron can be covered with "an impermeable surface coating" so that air and water don't reach it. I read him more about roses, "in case of die-back, shoots blacken;" he reads me more about rust.

"Which one do you guys want? Rust or roses?" he asks the customers.

"Rust," they say.

We keep reading back and forth till noon, then go to the used car dealer after that, then to the hardware store, where the old man buys a gallon of Rust Pruf. He applies it to his head, neck, and arms out in the alley. "Here, you put it on, too," he says. He tries Three-in-One Oil, deciding it's too expensive for Magda, whose terrible roses have grown considerably. She's got a whole garden in there. She tenderly nurses the stems and petals. She won't let Pa near.

I don't believe it's rust, though, and when he goes back to see his dolly at the bar, I read the directions on a canister of Ferti-Lome Rose Dust. "It says here I've gotta 'hold duster 12-18 inches' from you, Ma." She's sleeping. I don't talk loud. "You're 'the surface to be dusted.' Let's see, 'Apply Ferti-Lome Rose Dust in such a manner that a uniform, hardly visible coating results on both sides of foliage.'" I shake the can, sprinkle it out. Suddenly her rust turns white with powder. Ma's a beautiful, red rose who has only me to keep off the aphids, the dipterous leaf miners, or the two-spotted spiders.

A POSTCARD: SUPERIOR, WISCONSIN, pop. 28,000, has two, actually three things to set it apart. It has 1) the highest rate of alcoholism per capita for any city of its size in the country; 2) the "World's Largest Freshwater Sandbar," which is a long, sandy beach bordered by the lake on one side and a bay on the other; and 3) the "World's Largest Ore Docks," which are three in number, but only one in actual use. At nine o'clock on the night of the dusting and sprinkling, I get a phone call from someone who wishes to meet me behind the Whoop 'n Holler.

Now the rest of a word postcard: The N.P. ore dock, like the globe at the gas plant, stands about a mile from our house, but in another direction from the gas globe. From either side of the dock, long metal chutes, which are rusty like everything else, hang over the water. Railroad engineers once positioned locomotives over the chutes. Now there is a different sort of positioning going on below. In the old days, ore slid down the lowered chutes into the open holds of boats. It made a curious sound, an avalanche of ore against steel. On still summer nights, you'd hear the sound of commerce in the harbor, a sound I heard the night I "shipped out."

I was working for the old man, waiting on tables and booths until after midnight. I was, you might say to use a nautical term, a deckhand. This was three years ago. I was still in high school when this old sailor off of the *Mantodoc* came up. That was a Canadian vessel. You can tell by the "doc" of the name, which means Dominion of Canada.

"All ahead two-thirds, Mate?" he asked.

I didn't know what he meant, but he left money for me and a note: "Let me trim your jib."

He returned the next night. "All ahead—?"

"You own a car?" I asked. I was worried who would know if I left with him.

"I've got money and a rented car," he said.

"Do I have to sit in the bosun's chair?" I asked.

"We'll see about it, Mate?" he said.

"I need money and beer then."

"Steady as she goes, Mate," he said.

He said it again as he eased toward me in the back seat of a rental car under the N.P. ore dock. "Steady now ... steady as she goes. All ahead one-third?"

"All ahead," I repeated.

"Two-thirds then?"

"Two-thirds then."

It was the sound of commerce. I'd hear it again and again after that. It always left me crying, my heart broken. That was the start of my career on the lakes. Night after night now the ore carriers whistle departure and the tug responds.

Ma wasn't afflicted with aphids that night I first came home sorry for what I'd done with the Canadian seaman. She'd done this type of work herself out of a house at 314 John Avenue. I carried on tradition. I washed up, kissed her, went to sleep dreaming that someday there'd be no use for me, that, unprotected, my Heartbreak Hotel sign would fall away in the fog and be replaced by something else, a flower shop sign maybe. To have someone watch out for you in the world, that's what mattered, I kept thinking. I awoke at two when the old man rolled in singing, "O Canada." I didn't want to go it alone into the night, but I had Ma then and so didn't worry. As much as I hated Stan Harris, the old man, I loved Magda Harris, my mom.

THE OLD MAN CALLS HER "Hagda" and always has. His metallurgy book may be correct about her. I don't see it this way. I see her as a rose.

The rust follows the general form of her old, shapeless body. It rises for the mole on her neck and falls for the deep scar on her shoulder. Her voice has changed. It's become tinny. For two months, she's been giving orders.

"Tighten the lid on the pressure cooker," she says. I thought she was talking to me, thought she knew what I'd been doing with my nights.

"Yes, Hagda," the old man says.

"You emptied the vacuum cleaner bag lately? Are the dishes clean? You want an old woman to get up from her rust bed? Not on your life! I'm glad it's almost over."

EVERYTHING I TOUCH IS OILY. Sometimes, the old man forgets about moisture. He uses the steam iron, puts on the vaporizer, leaves water standing in the tub.

"Check the humidity in here," she says.

He understands the chemical process of corrosion, but he just huffs and argues and does nothing.

In Ma's rust-encased brain, she is shutting him out, turning her corroded back on him. But by doing it she's leaving me out, too. Her legs get red-rose marks.

"Don't do this, Ma. I'm unprotected. I don't have anyone to look after me," I tell her. "I don't want to be up on deck alone. I'm afraid of being a deckhand. Something bad is gonna happen to me."

Then these bronze circles appear on her which begin to fall off.

"Please, Ma, please," I say.

The fine dust we saw on her pillow appears everywhere. Her fingers are growing brittle. They rust and flatten. She can't walk far. "Be careful of road salt," I tell her in early November. When she strikes her hands together, they make a sound which infuriates Pa. She's not much to look at. Rusty parts fall off. Her voice sounds sharp and brittle as though it's coming through a tin aperture or horn, as through a steel pipe. "'tanley, brin' me the 'offee." He can hardly stand it that she won't allow him in her garden of roses. "Why should I? You were no goo't t' me (You were no good to me)," she says.

"Magda, I tried. I got you a nice, warm place here. See how nice. Isn't it something to be proud of? Heck, how long've we been together, Mag?"

"'ort' yea's."

"Yes, almost a golden anniversary coming up. Hang around a few more years, Mag! Why d'ya want to go this way? Who'm I gonna bring home beer to?"

"'ut sup, 'tanley Harris," she says. "'et me sleep!"

ONE DAY LATE IN LIFE, the old man becomes a philosopher. In all the bars on Tower Avenue and 3rd, he's heard of no others who are afflicted with rust, so he begins to search heaven and earth. "Why do you suppose this all is happening?" he asks.

In Heartbreak Hotel, he sits across a table from a guy who's soaking his thumbs in a bowl of water.

"Who are we?" Pa asks. I join the two men. "No, really. I need answers. Who are we?"

"Two drunks," the man says. His face is red. (Think of a postcard of a puffed and veined nose hanging from a guy's face like a magnificent, intricately patterned hive. His thumbs are discolored from hammer blows. One day he invited customers to hit his thumbs, so long as they bought him a beer.) "Have you heard about Magda Harris who used to work over at 314 John Avenue?" the man says.

"Don't you know that's my wife?" Pa says. As the man cradles his thumbs, Pa asks him, "Why do people suffer? Who oxidizes Magda and not, not … you, for instance?"

"I don't know any of it, but I ain't drunk and I know nobody'd give her a burial in her condition. I saw a chunk of metal on the street, a rusted-up fender. Is that what she's like?"

The thumb-and-hammer man goes with us to the dock. Some, but not us, would seek in religion the answers to such problems as why human beings must suffer on earth. The dock is a kind of spiritual place for the city and region. Out of this dock, ore used to go to rusting cities like East Chicago and Cleveland. We'd give these cities the raw goods for their blast furnaces.

A cinder path runs beneath the arched ceiling. Standing at one end, your view narrows to where the arches come together at the far end. It's an illusion Pa and I enjoy. When you look up at this ore palace, you think of churches in town whose ceilings are also meant to elevate the spirit. They have sacred paintings and lights made to look like stars on the ceiling; the docks have pigeons roosting in the ore pockets.

"Who's drawing all those broken hearts here?" the old man

asks. It's like someone who's been sitting in a parked car maybe has been counting them and keeping score. There are twenty-three broken hearts in all. Bobby Harris. Bobby Harris, the sign in town says.

In some places, the light filters down on us. It's a good thing most of the path is in shadows, so the old man can't see where my phone number is written in chalk on the walls. The slip hasn't frozen. Water laps at the sides of the dock.

"If she's gonna act that way, I'll revenge myself on earth," the old man says.

The thumb-and-hammer man says, "You know how much your heart and mind can take. You know that if your heart's made of iron, you need to keep it lubricated right every day. You know ... Look at my thumbs!"

I hear this conversation between the two of them drifting out over the water. The piece of ore stains my fingers when I pick it up. First, I draw a heart on the wall, then "Bobby Harris 394-5729."

We all walk back to Heartbreak Hotel. On the jukebox, Pa plays his favorite tune, "The Swamper's Revenge on the Windfall." "There ain't no rust where there's beer," he says. He drinks six cans of Royal Bohemian. "Oxidize me, boys! Sell me for scrap!" he says. They can't believe his story. He downs a shot of schnapps, a brandy and water, a bowl of beer. "This is my wife," he says. He bangs a tin ashtray on the table, puts one on his head. "'tanley, bring me 'ore hot 'offee 'ow!" He has another glass of beer, then one for the road.

AT HOME, MA IS FINALLY, willfully, rusting to death.

"Don't, Ma," I beg.

"G'night, son."

"Ma, fight it. Don't give in!" It's a deep, rusty sleep she falls into like no one on earth has ever known.

I run to Heartbreak Hotel. "C'mon," I say. I pull at his

jacket. As her last, few healthy cells succumb and rust extinguishes the light from her eyes, as her head and heart become totally oxidized, the old man gets a second wind. "C'mon, Pa. C'mon!" He consumes four more beers, a nightcap, and another one for the road. Then he decides on an eye-opener. "You son of a bitch," I tell him.

What remains on the couch for us to find at four A.M. is a thin red strip of what used to be my mother. The old man fidgets with his collar, then stares to where Ma's rusted arm is thrown back over her head as though pointing a finger at Pittsburgh or other Rust Belt cities. The old man is moved. Taking her in his arms, he hugs her and cries. He scratches himself on her rusty arms. He'll have to be more careful, he says.

The thumb-and-hammer man was right. No one will bury a person whose life has corroded. We leave her on the couch till we can think of what to do. It takes the old man two weeks to decide. "The hardest part will be getting her down there," he says.

Then one late afternoon he hauls the wagon out of the garage. He has been in the bar all day, and struggling with the wagon and with Ma helps to clear his head. "That's a fine girl, Mag. Here we are," he says. Embracing her brittle, blushing body, he realizes how unfair life can be. He stares deep into her rusty eyes. "There now," he says to soothe her.

What secrets could you tell me, Ma? What secrets of the deep, selfish pleasures of oxidation? Where have you gone, where do I look for you?

PA RUNS THE ROPE THROUGH a hole where her hip has rusted, then ties the rope around the wagon to offer some stability. One day, I think to myself, university archaeologists digging at the base of what looks like a temple or ore palace of some fantastic shape may find what they believe to be evidence of an age long disappeared, an age characterized by men who'd do anything, even smash their fingers, for a sip of beer. Pa looks at his own fingers. All there in fine shape. He wouldn't have to be like the thumb-and-hammer man.

"It wasn't bad enough that he humiliated her," I tell the same thumb-and-hammer man some days later, "then he had to *humidify* her."

"What else did he do?"

"Exposed her to road salt."

"What else?"

"Bathed her too often."

"Yeah? What was his motive?"

"To get beer money," I say.

"Now, kid," he says. "It's Bobby, ain't it? Your daddy's a fine man, as good a fellow as—"

"But he humidified her!"

"Kid, I'll tell you something I heard about you, Bobby. I heard about the docks. You better watch your tongue. Now you go home and listen well to your Papa, as good and kind a one as the day is long."

Pulling the wagon beside the railroad tracks, my old man stops to salvage a rusty bolt laying half-buried in weeds. Another time he pries out a hunk of iron ore fallen from a boxcar and tosses it in the wagon with his beloved. He'd have plenty to remember her by. He'll keep these things in his drawer, I think, maybe even pray to them. Some day when he's real old and living in a room behind Heartbreak Hotel, he'll pull out the rusted bolt and tell some visitor, "This is my good, dear wife who preceded me in death."

Now even the sun sinking through layers of industrial smoke over West Duluth looks old and rusty. "We've had a good life, ain't we, Mag?" the old man asks. "Sure we did. Things all worked out. Don't ya see, Mag, it's a wonderful, beautiful sunset to your life," he mutters to keep from sobbing. He can't cry. He's being careful of moisture.

But I, Bobby Harris, can't stop crying. I've got no one now, nothing but Heartbreak Hotel. I am left unprotected to hate his life, his sobbing, bellering life.

You'd be able to tell how deep she went by how long water kept rolling up to the surface. The old man lugs her to the edge. He wears gloves to protect himself from cuts and scratches. I, on the other hand, desire her violent, sharp edges to mark my arms.

He has hauled what passes for Ma all the way from home down the Great Northern tracks, then down the cinder path to the end of the dock—and nobody will do anything about it. ("He vaporized her," I told the thumb-and-hammer man. "He exposed her to relative humidity. He was the relative behind the humidity.")

Careful not to snag his clothes, the old man gives her one last heave and rolls her in. "I hate to see it happen like this," he says. The water in the slip is deep, for the wake of Ma's passing takes up one whole minute. Then there are bubbles. Pa dusts himself off as he mutters a prayer over the dear departed. To him she's become a rusty old hulk, nothing more. In his coat pocket, he rummages for a few remaining petals to scatter over the bay. That done, he mutters something else and strolls back to Heartbreak Hotel where he's left some change on the bar.

It's just me, the wagon, and the fog. As the sun sets, the fog rises with the moon. Night after night, month after month, it billows in. It dampens your face and sometimes obscures the mean edge of life around the warehouses and docks on lower 3rd. On some nights when it's really bad all you'll see on the entire street is a broken heart, or plenty of broken hearts ducking back into the doorsteps as you pass. Aching for love, I stand out among them. Drunks strolling by, sometimes a sailor, I'll whisper, "All ahead two-thirds?"

I've been hurt at it a few times. Unprotected things fall apart in the rain, I've found. A gentleman I met once had no transportation. We took the bus to the end of the line where he rang me off. Another time a sailor on the *Richfield* went Full Throttle when I'd asked for Reverse. Then Ma died. Then the elderly Canadian returned to trim me. "Steady ... steady," he implored. "Give me the steam ... Full ahead!" he cried, and it was too much for me and I got out of there without my five dollars pay.

I've broken my heart all over town. On every pillar of the docks, I've drawn broken hearts in ore dust. On every park bench in Superior, I've carved them with stones and knives: Bobby Harris Bobby Harris Bobby Harris.

The Moon of the Grass Fires

Above the flour mill it appeared as though the body of Jesus Christ hung in the fine waves of wheat dust. People would say it was an optical illusion created by the dust, but why not this reflection of Christ when twenty-four hours a day the mill refined wheat into the flour Catholic bakers use? From around the country, laity and nuns in the bakers' trade wrote letters saying what exceptional Eucharistic flour it was. Of course, St. Adalbert's Church used communion wafers made from wheat milled at The Fredericka, so there was also a customer base right in Joe Lesczyk's hometown.

Now retired, Joe Lesczynski (Lesczyk, his grandfather shortened the name when he came to America) could relax without worrying about the mill. For eight hours five days a week for forty years, he'd oiled motors, laid conduit, packed flour—done a dozen dusty chores at the mill. Seeing himself in the mirror, he shook his head sadly, thinking how he looked like an old man who'd slept in a perpetual blizzard all his life, which really isn't far from truth given northern Wisconsin's climate. However, it wasn't ice or snow but semolina dust come to the fine map of Joe Lesczyk's face much as the autumn frost settles in ravines and swamps and on the gardens and fields of East End. How many years since he was young? Joe Lesczyk wondered.

A week after his retirement the year before, an odd thing had happened to him. He'd come into possession of a church confessional, a plain, wooden, rectangular structure that stood five feet high, eight or nine feet long, perhaps four across. He got it when one of the Slovaks of the parish, the successful corner grocery store owner Mrs. Bendis, contributed money for a new confessional. This being Father Nowak's *Jubileusz kapłanstwa*, his Silver Jubilee Anniversary, what better gift than a more stylish confessional for the priest Nowak? Because Joe Lesczyk couldn't stand seeing the old one hauled off to an industrial waste landfill where the crucifix would poke out from demolition debris, he asked the parish council if he could have the confessional.

Sin is not light, of course. A confessional can weigh six hundred pounds or more. How difficult it was for the boys he hired to lift it into the rusty bed of a pickup truck. On the way down East Fourth Street to Joe Lesczyk's two-car garage, the purple confessional curtains danced gaily in the breeze. Then at the house, the boys slid the confessional out an inch at a time so they could get hold of it and carry it into the garage where they set it down in a corner.

Now that the confessional was "decommissioned" and he was alone with it, Joe Lesczyk, more contemplative in retirement, thought how for ninety years sinners—shadowy, immobile, pensive—knelt on these very kneelers waiting for one priest or another to slide open the wooden door to the screen separating penitent from confessor. Saturday after Saturday a priest sat in the lonely box.

Through almost his entire life, Joe Lesczyk had also knelt in this confessional on one side of which a placard read: CONFESSIONS IN POLISH HEARD HERE. Envy, covetousness, lewd thoughts, taking God's name in vain; so often he'd burdened the old priest Father Marciniak and later his replacement Father Nowak with his sins. What could they have thought? True, a cloth screen separated them from him and, true, the light in the confessional booth was dim, but the priests still knew which parishioner was here to whisper of spiritual failure. Now that he was proud owner of a confessional it seemed to him as if he could reclaim his sins from it.

"Mister, they shoulda never painted this thing," a furniture stripper, a non-Catholic, told him a few days later. "Looks like they had good paint back then. Makes it hard to get it off when the paint's so good." At first the refinisher thought it was a kids' playhouse. He wanted $750 to haul the confessional out of Joe's garage to his shop, there to suspend it in a vat of paint remover for as long as it took to strip off the paint. "It'll be the first and last I'll ever do," he said. "A lot of work. I suppose you Catholics would say there's sin in the walls, even in the nails."

The real sin was how much the refinisher would charge, Joe Lesczyk thought. That's when he decided to hire a couple of the neighborhood boys, the movers, to strip the whole thing down, then put on a good coat of lacquer to enhance the beautiful wood he imagined lay beneath. They could brush on paint remover, scrape off the layers of enamel with a putty knife, and so could he when he felt up to it. Working a few days a week, in six months they'd have a good conversation piece. It'd be a retirement project. It would be cheaper this way, too: the economical, hands-on way of cleaning off the yellowing past of sinfulness that had formed a patina on the walls. If the garage got too cluttered, maybe in time he would donate the fresh, clean confessional to the historical society.

When he'd taken down the two curtains plus the one that'd hidden the priest in the center part, the phone rang. He'd left the living room window and the front door open so he could hear the phone.

"I'm fine," he said when his wife asked. She was in Florida visiting their daughter Meg. "Everything okay in St. Petersburg?"

"We're doing great. You okay, Joe?"

"I'm okay. Meg okay?"

"We're fine," said Barbara.

"Guess what? I'm working on our retirement project."

"What?"

"You remember. From St. Adalbert's. I asked a furniture stripper to quote me a price."

"I'm starting to worry about you. Are you feeling okay?" said his wife.

"I feel great. The thing is the confessional," he said. "We can confess to each other. I'm going to try some paint remover myself on it in a minute."

"Will you call me later? Please tell me you're all right."

"Sure I'll call," he said. "And I couldn't be happier. Hey, I'm retired. If there's something you want to confess, let me know, Barbara."

"This comes as a surprise. I'll call you when the news sinks in. What does anyone need a confessional for?"

"To find out about ourselves and why we sin," he said.

"Don't learn too much,"she said. "Wait 'til I get back."

AFTER THE FIRST HOUR OF stripping paint, he realized the job was bigger than he thought. The confessional seemed larger without curtains. It had been built big to accommodate the gruff workers with mortal sins needing confession and absolution—railroad car knockers, ore punchers, sailors off the lake boats, millhands guilty of terrible deeds. All those years of sinning. He worked for another hour with cloth and scraper, then, cautioning himself to slow down, reminding himself he was retired, he sat awhile in the priest's side of the confessional. He recalled some of the parishioners who'd knelt to confess: Mrs. Pilsudski, Michael Zimski, the Milszewski boy with a Purple Heart, Louie Stefanko. He recalled how rarely Mr. Zielinski observed the Fourth Commandment, how it was whispered that Mr. Dzelak was remiss in areas of life covered by the Fifth Commandment, how Mr. Marsolek, Mr. Novazinski, and Mrs. Petruska, the school teacher, were remiss in the Sixth Commandment. As though someone were in the garage to hear him, he called out his parents' names as among the sinners. What a silly thing, to sit alone in retirement and say names aloud to yourself. He repeated relatives' names, repeated his own and his wife's names, but when he said "Mother" again as though asking her something he'd wondered about, he broke the stillness in such a way that he felt it would be better to leave the confessor's center part to kneel in one of the penitent's boxes. "Bless me, Father, for I have sinned ...," he said and began, as a kind of Examination of Conscience, to retell the passions of his and his mother's lives.

He remembered her in the kitchen years before saying, "Do it for me, Joseph." Over half a century earlier, he'd knelt in the back pew of St. Adalbert's Church and wondered, "Have I neglected my parents in their necessity?"

"Dad says no. I'm not supposed to go to the drugstore for you. He says the stuff makes you sick and crazy."

"You can do it for me," she implored. He was nine, ten perhaps. Life had passed so quickly since then. Now he himself was old.

"For me, Joe. Run an errand for your mom. Sure, you won't mind doing that. You're a good boy."

It was a fine afternoon this time she'd wanted her Asthmador Powder. He was on his way to play football with the neighbor boys. "Just take your bike and run an errand to the drugstore for me," she said.

"No, I can't, Mother."

Why she hadn't pulled on a sweater and walked to the store herself, he couldn't understand. "Please, Joe, go after it for me?" she asked again. "Then deliver this note to Mr. Mrozek."

How blue the sky was back then but for that slight smoke haze in the distance. Every autumn, people set fire to their vacant lots and fields and burned their piles of leaves.

Now not so many years later, needing to leave the confessional, he decided to rake leaves beneath the apple tree for an hour. Over the yards and fields, daydreams hovered in the smoke. He remembered his mother in the kitchen wearing her maroon bathrobe with its sagging pockets, her hair uncombed. Though not intending to startle her son, to steady herself, she grabbed his shirtsleeves. He kept telling her he didn't want to go to the store for her or to deliver any messages to the neighbor, an accordion player whose house lay across and down a dusty alley. "I won't go over to Buck's Mrozek's," Joe Lesczyk said to his mother. "No more requests for Buck Mrozek." He said it now as he picked an apple from the tree.

During the warmer months, you could hear Buck Mrozek practicing his music. He left the kitchen window open or practiced the accordion right out in his backyard. Everyone loved him, especially Joe Lescyzk's mother. During an evening, you never heard the same song twice, and, with his expensive accordion and the finest Frankie Yankovic sheet music collection in northern Wisconsin, Buck took requests. Even Joe himself liked to hear him play. Seeing the neighbor boy admiring him, Buck would smile, break into "She's Too Fat Polka" in honor of one of the Polish ladies passing down the alley, and shout over the music " Hoo-yaa-yaa." A "hoo-hoo-hoo" or "yoo-hoo-hoo" could be heard from neighboring houses.

Now years later with the moon rising over the smoke, the retired millhand expected the music but instead heard the phone ring.

"Dad, is that you?" the voice said. "Sorry we haven't talked. I've been busy," Meg said.

"I was outside," he said.

"How's retirement?"

"Fine. I was outside being retired. Guess what? I'm having an apple."

"Wish I could join you. Aren't they good?"

"How's your ma?"

"Fine. We're watching the baby."

"Did I tell you I'm having an apple from your grandfather's tree?"

"Enjoy it. You deserve it."

"The moon's out early. The air smells like fire. It's people burning their leaves. It's the best time of year. Remember autumn evenings in Superior?"

"You deserve autumn," Meg said. "You worked hard all your life to get there. Look at how our time's gone. I've gotta go. I've gotta check on the baby."

She hung up.

"Meg?" he said, noticing as he sat with the receiver in his hand that the moon was following him into the room.

Its light stayed with him until 10:30, until midnight. When he arose at 2:30 and went downstairs, there it was: the moon. Opening the living-room drapes, he watched the apple tree throw its moonlit shadows over the strange, yellow-silver night.

Years ago he'd stood in the kitchen, his mother balancing herself against the table. On a plate she'd pour a little pile of the green powder she'd light with a stick match. She leaned forward to inhale the gray-green smoke. Stumbling sideways, she'd say, "Deliver the note. I'm out. Go to the store for your mother, Joey."

He'd thrown on his jacket … was standing in the back shed that led into the kitchen. His father was at work.

"He doesn't want me to, Dad doesn't," he'd said.

It was who might have seen her, he thought, that's why his mother, a married woman, a Catholic, wouldn't carry a note with a polka request down the alley or get the can of Asthmador Powder for her breathing. Stumbling like that, she couldn't walk to the drugstore. None of it made sense back then when his father asked the druggist not to sell her the medication. "Don't go for her if she asks you to, Joe, and I'm at work," his dad said.

"Oh, please, Joey," she'd say. "I'm gonna fall down on this floor and get very sick."

"I can't help you," he'd tell her. "It's a sin for me to run your errands."

"Hug me," she'd say and give him seventy-five cents for her Asthmador Powder.

Later when he sat across from her at the kitchen table, thick smoke rose about her face and she was calm. "Did you go across the alley for me, too? Did you tell Buck to play 'The East End Polka'?"

"I told him."

"What did he say?"

"He said, 'Yoo-hoo-hoo.'"

"Not 'hoo-hoo-hoo'? Are you sure you're not mixed up?"

"No. You're the one that's mixed up," Joe said.

"Don't speak like that to your mother. Haven't you learned anything from your catechism? What does it say about respect for our parents, about not abandoning our mothers in their necessity?"

His mother started getting crazy again, talking faster. "Examine your conscience. Study the *Baltimore Catechism*. Don't fail me in life. Buck's famous for 'The East End Polka.' He could've toured with 'Whoopee John' Wilfahrt or played with Dick Contino's band. Buck's a good, decent neighbor. What do you know about polka? You come here. Ma wants you to dance with her."

Clapping her hands, she got up a polka beat. "You sing along, Joey. Buck wrote this song,

> *She lives in East End,*
> *I live in Nord' End.*
> *I work the shipyard,*
> *She works the bakery.*
> *When we're in East End—*

Come on, Joey!"

"'We dance the polka,'" he sang the next line and the

next as she swayed so hard he felt sick to his stomach watching her.

When she polkaed nearer to him, he hid from her on the back porch. That day for the first time he noticed that his mother's dress, too tight about the stomach, had spots on the sleeves and that her arms sagged with flesh. Her hair had started to gray. He watched her dance until she slumped down in a chair, laid her head on the table, and cried. She'd had a catharsis, a kind of polka catharsis.

"'We dance the polka. Oh, aren't we happy?'" he sang softly to her from the porch after five minutes.

"No, we aren't happy unless you run her errands for your mother, Joey, just across the alley with requests. You've gotta go fast before Dad gets home."

"I won't fail you in your necessity," Joe said.

STELLA LESCZYK'S BREATHING NEVER improved. She'd used the smoking powder a long time before a new doctor made her stop. "There's belladonna in it," the doctor told his father. Sometimes Joe couldn't remember the name—belladonna—but he remembered how his father was furious with his wife when he came home the day she was dancing. Joe remembered her begging her husband not to be angry, remembered her saying she couldn't help it if she was addicted. She'd make his favorite noodle dish if he wouldn't be angry. "It's the asthma powder that gets her," Mr. Lesczyk was telling his son. "It has nothing to do with polka. She shouldn't give polka a bad name."

Years later—Mr. Lesczyk having preceded her in death—she lay in a hospital, heart enlarged from the asthma. Face flushed from coughing, she wanted Joe to hold her hand. Instead, he wiped her mouth with a napkin, threw the napkin in the wastebasket, then stepped out. When he did, her coughing stopped. In the hospital waiting room, a now ancient Buck Mrozek sat with his accordion. He showed Joe a new arrangement of an old standard. It was as if Buck was seeking the right combination of words and polka music to keep Mrs. Lesczyk alive. She was his biggest fan; he was the undisputed polka king of East End. "Please get better, Ma," Joe, her son, was pleading, but that day she died, and he, Joe Lesczyk of Fredericka Flour, had to tell Buck to put away the accordion. Some years later, the King himself, Buck Mrozek, died, leaving his music to his son.

Now with the moon over the harvest fields, Joe Lesczyk thought of calling his wife in Florida, but when he looked at the clock, it was 3 A.M.

Despite his joy, each day brought sadness, for he was understanding the mystery and pain of life. When the breezes blew, the maple tree in the yard shimmered in sunlight—a delicate time in his retirement. When he looked at the confessional, he noticed how the wood, though covered with paint long ago, was still smooth to the touch. The old people were dead, but here he stayed thinking of them, their lives growing into the one big mystery that included the image of Christ reflected in dust over the mill.

Not much was said about Stella Lesczyk's addiction. She'd stopped using the smoking powder, and no one talked about it, and to her son it was a memory. Dreams, myster—…, *memories*; they get mixed up.

"Bless me, Father, for I have sinned," he said—the opening words of the "Form of Confession." Instead of kneeling in the confessional, he decided to look in an old dresser in the garage for the broken dinner plate she used for a smoking dish. He wished to have it, the burnt part, to smell the thick, bitter dreams of childhood. "I'm home," he was saying out loud. No one was there to hear. "I'll be back in the house in a moment. Do you want anything? I'm practicing the 'Form of Confession' out here in the garage. 'Bless me, Father, for I have sinned.' It's the confessional all of you knelt in."

He spoke aloud to his parents, to his aunts and uncles. He told them he had more time to think of them now. He wondered if they could hear him. "I'm in the garage," he told their ghosts again. "I never wanted to disappoint any of you," he said as if, so long after she died, his mother could hear him. Christ in the mystery of confession, in the mystery of the Eucharist, knew what was happening to Joseph Lesczyk in his retirement.

"Please, Joe-Sweetie. Take a minute to go to the drugstore for me on your bike."

"No," said Joe Lesczyk, who thought he heard a polka. "No," he said again now in retirement.

MEMORY WAS HIS RETIREMENT problem—not health concerns, not financial worries. Remembering was the problem. He'd rake leaves, then dwell on autumn and winter themes. As he waited for the moon, he knew nobody in his family ever died in summer. They died when it was bitter cold and cemetery workers had to plow the snow, then thaw a section of ground with torches so they could dig in it. His mother died on All Souls' Day, his father in an earlier year eight days before Christmas. Both times Joe Lesczyk, Fredericka employee, came to confession. To receive the Holy Eucharist whose wheat he milled, he had to be pure of heart. In winter were deaths and disappointments. During the bitter season a man counts on them. But not in summer. No summer disappointments. He'd made it to retirement.

Now fall had come and with it the moon of the grass fires. He'd often wondered how long to defer payment on the past. Then this evening, the moon, bigger than any this autumn, rose right down at the end of the street, where it insisted on staying. He'd been raking leaves, listening to music drift over the air (the high school band preparing for homecoming, he thought) when, just as he was about to forgive his mother for requesting "The East End Polka" so often all those years, the yellow-eyed moon took his breath away.

It was so aged and huge, that harvest moon intruding at the end of Fourth Street, that he started walking toward it as if it had something special to tell him. The neighbors wondered why he was heading away from the church and the flour mill where they'd seen him coming and going all his life. Now they saw him head in this new direction because a light breeze that carries the flour dust with it had come up; he wasn't walking against it but with the breeze. If you are a believer, you'd say, perhaps only a little fancifully, that he was walking in the direction of the holy garments of Jesus Christ, enjoying the protection of His gentle shimmering robes. Almost imperceptibly at first, the amber dust from wheat that would eventually be made into Christ's Body in the Eucharist settled onto the former millhand.

"Hello, Joe Lesczyk," people called as they passed. "How's retirement?"

"Fine," he answered. Then, with his eyes on the moon, he said, "Look how old the moon grows. What mysteries! It shined on Jesus in the garden, on Jesus on the cross. Lord, forgive us all."

A group of boys started following him on bikes the way Joe Lesczyk, on his own bicycle as a youth, would have followed someone like him on an autumn evening. They were good children. Trained by the nuns at St. Adalbert's, they knew both their "Form of Confession" and their "Prayers for the Adoration of the Eucharist." Eventually some of their parents joined them.

"You're full of dust, Mr. Lesczyk," they called to him.

When he stopped and made the sign of the cross on his forehead he said, "Yes, I finally see that."

At the abandoned ore dock, he stopped again with his flock. From there you can plainly observe what the moon of the grass fires illuminates—a valley, a railroad trestle, a Left-Handed River. Joe Lesczyk saw his entire life, remembered his hard-working father, remembered the pain his mother'd caused them.

Now a few curious boys rode closer to him so they could touch his sleeve to watch dust rise. "You're *really* full of dust now, Mr. Lesczyk," they said. In the soft breeze, the wheat dust fell lightly on all of them, the amber dust of the Lamb of God.

"May the Body of Our Lord, Jesus Christ, keep our souls," he said.

Hearing the retired millhand, the boys began to notice the dust on themselves; but, because they were young and hadn't seen much of life's sorrows, at first they made no connection between themselves, Joe Lesczyk, and the Body of Our Savior on this beautiful autumn evening.

THE ABSOLUTION OF HEDDA BORSKI

I have prepared the bread and cotton when the priest arrives a little after eight. He's said Mass at St. Adalbert's and come over. We have coffee.

"Your house looks very nice," he says. "Do you live downstairs? Where's your sister?"

"In her bedroom." I hear her up there shuffling things on the nightstand. "She takes medicine for an enlarged heart," I tell him. "She hasn't been downstairs in years."

"My heart can't take it," she says when we're halfway up the stairs to see her. "Tell him that, too, Julia! I hear you coming."

I carry up the table with the candlesticks, bread, and cotton and leave it outside her door. I whisper to the priest how I've heard her stories so often I have to cut her off midway to save my sanity. "This time she'll tell you how a nice young man broke her heart. But, Father, remember it's partly the medicine that confuses her. Everything's jumbled up in her head."

Entering the room, he notices the picture of the Sacred Heart of Jesus. Then Hedda starts in exactly as I said she would.

"I know the one who broke my heart," she says.

Her nightstand is filled with pills and water glasses. Gray curls fall out from her nightcap. She wears her glasses, and the counterpane is pulled up and tucked under her arm. Her rosary hangs from the bedpost.

"Hedda, Father O'Donnell is here."

We're already beside her when she answers, "Come in!" She reaches for the priest's hands. "You must know I wanted the baby, Father."

"Hedda!" I say. "Stop it. No more tall tales."

"Yes, Father. Now that you've seen an old lady in her night-cap, may I tell you something?"

"Go on," the priest says. So she proceeds with her favorite story.

"The river's name is 'Left-Handed.' A Left-Handed River. Do you know why we call it that?"

"Indians called it that," I say.

"Don't intrude, Julia," she says.

"But, Dear, I want to get you moving. Father O'Donnell doesn't have all morning," I say.

"Well, as they canoed in from Lake Superior, the Indians saw a river to the left. '*Nemadji*' means 'Left-Handed.' Another Ojibwe word is '*Onawe*.' It means 'Awake, Beloved.' Those are the two words I know."

"In seminary, we studied Latin," the priest says.

"Hurry," I tell Hedda. "Let's get to the point."

"Well, I have a rather startling story," my sister says. "I hope you'll believe it on faith, Father, as you believe in the Trinity on faith. If you're willing to, then believe me when I say that my dead child returned once—from the dead, I tell you—and even muttered in his sleep when he opened his eyes a minute. He was a wonderful, silent, sleeping child whose dreams no doubt were pleasant for him. Are you able to believe that human beings return after death to us and sometimes sleep in the world for months, even years?"

Father O'Donnell takes the chair by her bed. He doesn't seem the least startled by her story. Perhaps, then, his imagination is large enough to listen to what she will tell him, I think.

"This man who made me pregnant and broke my heart," Hedda says, "between us, there'd been certain difficulties. He was a stronger person than I. I found out about my weak heart where a sidewalk ends at the edge of town. That's where he told me he was married and had a nice house. He was always one-up on me, this man, this lover. 'I was sure you weren't a denier, a person to say no,' I told him when it was all over. 'But I guess your marriage complicated matters for us. Such pain does happen, I see.'"

"Yes, I've seen it," says the priest.

"Now that we're so intimate, Father, do you want to know more disappointments I've suffered through, more crises of faith? It's easy to understand how they've occurred. Where was the confessor to hear what I'd done? My faith had deserted me. I was very much alone, so what could I do in turn but abandon my God?" She points to the picture of the Sacred Heart. "For me, it was either faith in God or earthly love, and I chose what I needed at the moment. It was Christ's heart or mine on earth that I had to keep from breaking."

Now I bother my sister to interrupt her. "Take your pill. Here's water." She takes the pill from her hand, sips the water. "Too many pills!" she says.

Outside, the city buses roar down West Third Street; in the distance, horns and sirens blare. The bright, dry morning is perfect for early spring. Everywhere children outdoors will be happy, I think. In the school yard across the street, they laugh and run about. The Sisters of St. Joseph of the Third Order of St. Francis have them singing Easter songs a month early, songs which drift in through the window with the sun.

The priest helps Hedda put down the glass. He smoothes her pillow, guides her head back. "You know," he says, "life's big events are pretty easily counted, I've come to see; four or five passionate moments to mark the years. I count my First Communion, Ordination to the priesthood, and first Mass, my mother's death and two or three other important events as marking the sum of my life. Perhaps they've been fewer for you, but just as important. Is there anything else you must tell me?"

"No, Father."

"Then, Hedda, having heard your confession, that you

have experienced a loss of faith, I want to say to you in Latin, *Ego to absolvo ...* Go and sin no more."

"Don't absolve me of anything yet, Father," she says. "The child lived in my womb for fifteen weeks. Do you understand? The baby disappeared before it was born. Don't look for it out there on the playground. I have looked for years. My lover sat in the waiting room of a hotel, then excused himself to buy some winter pants. When he returned it was over. The baby was gone. 'You could've sat with me,' I said. He unwrapped the new pants.

"In another hotel, a little more expensive one, I lay awake. He stayed a day on business, then went home to try on the pants again. Left to myself, I stared at the ceiling. It was raining outside. I guessed it would be for a month. Now it had started raining through the ceiling. I lay on the bed in the rain which came in around the ceiling light, then spread to the corners until, finally, the whole ceiling was raining. But I rested. I was not so weak the morning after the loss of my child, but I was sick and worried over what I'd done. That was the start of my incompleteness. The rain stopped but the thunder didn't. I lay in the wet room thinking. And where was he but home in his new pants as I lowered myself into the bathtub which had those claw feet on it. As I dreamt of my child in this mean hotel, I wept. Taking the train home, I made it in time for work the next day.

"'You were crazy to think it'd work out. It was impractical,' he said when we met again.

"'Angelo, Angelo,' I said, 'how often you deceived me.'"

That happened to Hedda forty years ago, I think.

"Father, I do what I can to keep Hedda's room fresh," I say. "In warm weather, I keep the windows open, though not too much. The sound of children hurts her. She takes Inderal for her heart. Sometimes she has breathing problems. I used to keep fresh flowers in the room, didn't I, but they bothered your breathing, Hedda, didn't they? Ten years is a long time to live in one room and not move about the house, so I do what I can for her, Father. I bring up the radio or change the lampshade for day or evening use. She prefers the rose-colored one at night. I also keep her water glass full. This room, you'll see, has plain wallpaper. Sometimes I think patterned paper would give her more to look at."

I don't know how we've spent the hours, I think, but it's suddenly close to noon. We've all been sitting here, dreaming, Hedda staring at the ceiling. The alarm clock's ticking must have softened the morning sadness, calming us all.

"Has she told you the story of the odd, wandering family?" I ask.

"No," Father says.

"I want to make sure she doesn't repeat herself the way she does with me."

"Please feel free to go on," Father O'Donnell says.

"Well, let me begin for her," I say. "It's startling, a truly startling coincidence, but that very same week she lost her baby in the hotel room, another child came into her life. You'll never believe this, Father. It will take great faith to believe it. He was a member of a pious family of travelers who bowed their heads before they ate," I tell him. "Hedda has told me often how they'd taken a table at the place where she worked during the trouble in her life. She was a waitress at the Lake Shore Café. Until the boy dropped a piece of bread or a biscuit from the table, the family had been eating quietly with no problems. Then came a stir. 'You know better,' the man beside him said. Hedda and I presume it was the boy's father. Anyway, he slapped the child's wrist. The boy forgot to kiss the bread he'd picked up from the floor. This must have been the family's custom, to show how precious bread is. You could see they were tired, Hedda has always said, and that the man did not slap him in anger. The child cried, then fell asleep on the man's shoulder. They were all so tired from traveling, I think."

"That boy renewed himself," Hedda breaks in. "If you could've seen it, the love between them all ... how without fear he put his head on his father's shoulder, even though the father had corrected his behavior. The child knew where affection could be expected to come from. You could never count on me like that," Hedda says. Pulling back the curtain, she gazes out the window. "All of them but the boy got up when they were done. He rested his head against the back of the chair and slept. I whispered, 'Awake, Beloved.' I couldn't look at him long, for I had to work in the kitchen. When I returned and he was there, it dawned on me—"

"Father O'Donnell, they'd paid and left," I say.

"Walked out on their son?"

"Yes, certainly," says Hedda. She seems to be gathering strength from recalling it. "And he was a fine boy, Father. His hair was soft and brown. White down appeared at his temples. Though his face looked as if he'd known the world many years, there was nothing harsh about it. His lips were so smooth. His wise head bent forward like my own child's would have been in the same position if he was alive in me. Those rainy days— what had I done? It was hard believing my own baby had gone away. And now this ... Give me my pills, Julia!"

I do, Theolair, which she must take several times a day. Her difficulty breathing causes her heart to swell. Her poor heart works hard, the doctors say. To them everything's physical. But how do we know it's not bursting for other reasons?

The pill settled, she breathes normally again. She clears her throat, looks at the priest. "My losses grip me," she says. "Except for Julia, I have been alone for forty years. Just me, Julia, and the Trinity, a different Trinity from the one you worship, I'm afraid, Father. That evening, the sleeping child was abandoned I had to return to the kitchen. The other waitresses and some of the cooks huddled around him. Customers came by to gawk.

As he slept, some of them touched his hands or his hair. It'd begun raining. Where was his family? I wondered. Could they have left one so helpless, so simple and helpless? Was my own unborn child dreaming of me in his loneliness? Was it coincidence they'd come so soon apart? Was it God's design?"

"Stop a minute, Hedda," I tell her. "It was Christian of her to look after him so well while he was there in the restaurant, wasn't it, Father?"

"Yes, I think it was," the priest replies. "To abandon a child like that!"

"And the faith she exercised watching over this ... sleep, didn't it mitigate her own sin?"

"Perhaps."

"And you, Father, do you accept on faith that anyone could sleep this long?"

"Well, strange things happen in life, and we must have faith to find the truth of what is revealed to us. What harm is there believing somebody can sleep an hour or two in a restaurant? It's no question of spiritual faith."

"But that's just it! She says it was a *year*, not an hour he slept alone."

"It puzzles me that here memory fails when I can remember all else," Hedda says. "He came so soon after my loss—that's maybe why I'm so confused about him, whether he stayed an hour, half a year, a year."

"It's okay," I say, trying to calm her. I look at the priest. But Hedda starts in again. "Yes, perhaps winter and spring were short ... and summer never came, and there was no fall. Say that year you could count autumn weather in minutes, then the snow fell. An hour, a year, what difference? Maybe to me a year was like an hour that time. You know how, when you look back, sometimes your entire life seems to have been no longer than a few ill-chosen moments. Well, why not this? Why couldn't this happen?" Hedda asks.

She pauses a minute as if to collect her thoughts.

"They'd left him to my care," she says. "They'd extended their goodness by trusting someone who looked as though she'd allow no harm to visit a sleeping child. Do you see the irony? The boss of course thought it was great. His business doubled. People were coming in to eat and look at the sleeping boy in the chair. I'd wipe his face with a damp cloth and sit beside him when I wasn't busy. The boss was good that way. After hours, I would try to hold the boy before I went home. Having looked after him when I could during the day, I'd gone home long after midnight. I'd see his face looking out at me from cars parked in the rain. At home as I looked in the mirror, I'd see him over my shoulder in the corner of the room, just sitting sleeping with his head bowed. In my sleep, I saw him crying. When his mother finally did return, she made nothing special of all this. 'It's happened before,' I remember her saying. 'We hope he hasn't been trouble.' She threw her coat around the boy's shoulders and guided him out of the restaurant. 'We hope he hasn't been trouble ...' That and nothing more and they were gone."

Hedda looks up, as if she hates to return from the comfort of dreams. Over the past forty years, nothing has counted but her losses.

"So, Father, I set my clock to dream of resurrection—and withdrew. Though I continued to search the playground of St. Adalbert's School, nothing came of it. Thankfully, I didn't end up downstairs in the house. My heart couldn't take climbing up here to look out. I can see fine from here in this room." She points from her bed to the window and the children of St. Adalbert's playing below on this sunny day in spring. "I keep looking for my son."

"It's important for her to look out," I say.

"You know," she says, "the town suits me fine. East-side streets are named West Third or West Cedar. Our street is.

When they founded the town, the roads laid down a half-mile from the first houses were west-side streets. But the town expanded from its origins, so what is now the east-side has old, west-side street numbers in place. How things pass me by, Father O Donnell, how I'm stuck here on West Third. Forty years I've worshipped the wrong Trinity, a baby fifteen weeks in my womb, a sleeping boy of about twelve or thirteen, and I, Hedda Borski, a recluse now dying, who almost gave birth. I was the third member of the Trinity."

She is quiet for a moment. At such times, the alarm clock's ticking seems louder than ever.

"There's been talk of straightening the river," she says suddenly. "Next fall they'll straighten and lengthen it, making it a right-handed river, if you can imagine that. To do so, they'll bring a bulldozer and barge upriver, then dredge a course for the river through the island into the bay."

"West-side streets are becoming east-side streets, too," says the priest to console her. "Everything is getting restored to how it was. We're expecting new days."

She looks around at us, at the sunlight on the curtain, at the painting on the wall. Our Blessed Jesus points to His heart, a very sacred heart. Much too big to be contained in His bosom, it rises outside of His body in flames.

"No, he wasn't. No trouble at all," she begins again. "Quiet. Never troublesome, my child slept, dreamt the whole time with head bent forward, the wise look on his face. Such a baby you've never seen. I fed him, carried him in the rain, left him in the city. The sleeper, too. I remember the boy. If I set the clock on the bureau, Father, it'll be my time before long. I've lived long enough. I want to join God's Holy Trinity. Let me think that I was no denier and that somewhere the sleeping boy naps in a chair in the afternoon sun. Allow me to dream that my poor, sleeping son is still coming back the first hour I hear steam shovels down by the river. Please, dear God, allow me the deceptions I can summon now that I have faith."

"*Ego te absolvo*," the priest says again. He whispers to me, "Even if she is wrong, do you condemn the heart's last stirrings, Julia?"

"It's raining," Hedda says. She's sighing.

"Hurry," Father says, "light the candles." Then I know. He begins his prayers. In the hall, I have the bread and salt, the six balls of cotton to anoint her with.

"*Confiteor Deo omnipotenti . . .*" She joins him, "I confess to Almighty God, to Blessed Mary, ever Virgin, to Blessed Michael the Archangel, to Blessed John the Baptist, to the Holy Apostles Peter and Paul, and to all the Saints, that I have sinned exceedingly in thought, word and deed . . ."

"*Mea culpa, mea culpa, mea maxima culpa,*" he says as he strikes his breast. "*Idea precor beatam Mariam semper Virginem . . .*"

She follows him, "I beseech Blessed Mary, ever Virgin, Blessed Michael the Archangel, Blessed John the Baptist, the Holy Apostles Peter and Paul, and all the Saints, and you, Father, to pray for me."

"May almighty God have mercy on you, forgive you your sins, and bring you to life everlasting," he says. But she does not answer.

"My unborn child," she says after a moment. She tries taking the priest's hands. "Don't forget my baby of fifteen weeks. I won't leave him again."

But out on the playground, children's shrieks of joy drown her out, and we can't hear. They're so happy it's nice out.

"It makes the ceiling wet, the rain," Hedda says louder, as though frantic now to speak. "Don't leave him out there."

She seems to struggle with the rain we can't see. Across Third Street, the Sisters of St. Adalbert's ring the school bell. Children's voices pour in through the window with the sunlight. They are going into the building for the last time in Hedda's life.

"He's drowning!"

Father uncovers her hands and feet. Then we hurry to bring in the table with the white linen cloth and accessories. He will give her Last Rites. I stop for a moment to adore the Sacred Heart. It bursts from Christ's garments, a heart too large for Its body and all in flames. He is showing It to us. What is Its message? What fits the heart's wanting? I can't make out what It is saying to us. When I look again, Hedda's gone. Her head has slipped forward to her chest, eyes gazing nowhere if not at her own broken heart. Perhaps now she has gone to join the sleeper and her very own son. I think how it doesn't matter if I close her eyes to the sunlight.

"Blessed is the Holy Trinity and undivided Unity," Father O'Donnell is saying. He stands riffling through the pages of his book for appropriate prayers. He cannot seem to give up doing this and prays well on toward three o'clock as though embarrassed about sending her away in the rain.

CHILDREN OF STRANGERS

Ralph and Josie Slipkowski live on East Third Street in a blue bungalow with white trim. They have a brass doorknob and an American eagle door knocker which no one uses. Next to the door in summer a planter full of petunias cheers things up. A beautiful sugar maple also grows in their yard in Superior, Wisconsin, a railroad and port city whose motto, "Superior—Where Rail Meets Sail," was coined during a Chamber of Commerce meeting at the Androy Hotel on Tower Avenue. Ralph Slipkowski trims and waters his lawn. With knife and spade, he edges a border along the sidewalk so no weeds grow there. When Josephine needs emotional support, when she starts doubting the purpose of life, Ralph is around for her. Most people wouldn't believe anyone living in a well-kept house, whose appearance its owners take pride in preserving, would be so uncertain in life. Houses like the Slipkowskis' should project their owners' stability and be signatures of the well-kept existence—and Josie and Ralph's house is a modern, two-bedroom bungalow.

Examining themselves in the living room mirror, they see two people in decline. Ralph's been spending a lot of time in rooms with mirrors. This night, Josephine arranges her hair, her husband his tie. Actually, only Josie understands what's occurring around her. She sees no very good future for herself. Something's causing her to doubt again. She thinks of herself as being on the verge of time, the edge of time, though she never speaks of it this way. Poor Ralph doesn't see what's going on, Josie thinks. He's missing what stands right here before him in the mirror or outside on the street. Ralph has been kind and thoughtful. So, too, have the kids. But he doesn't see what's going on, she thinks. He has nothing to fear; he can't read the signs in the mirror.

"You can tell really good, expensive mirrors by placing a fingertip to the glass," he says. "There'll be an eighth-inch, maybe more, reflected from where your fingertip touches the glass to where the reflected one begins. Cheap mirrors don't reflect as deep as expensive ones. Expensive mirrors express a person better."

The oak dresser with Ralph and Josie's most expensive mirror stands in a house on an elm-lined street of houses which were kept up once, but now grow shabby. When they aren't painted, when little things go wrong, houses deteriorate. They've gotten so because people in Superior are out of work. The cold, rainy, foggy weather in summer only makes matters worse for the people and their houses, but not Ralph Slipkowski's house, for even in retirement, he's a tireless, meticulous worker, especially in a room with mirrors. The mirror on the oak dresser stands like a heart at the center of the house.

THE NUNS RESIDE TWO MILES from Ralph and Josie's. *Szkoła Wojciecha* means "Albert" or "Adalbert School." The pupils have names like Maretski, Mizinski, Symczyk, Lalko, and Urbaniak. In school, they are more sober and industrious than their parents. Stanislaus Wysinski, the Slipkowskis' neighbor, has taken his boy to the window, pointed to railroad section hands toiling on the Great Northern spur track, and said, "You straighten out in school, or when you're eighteen, you'll be hiding sand under railroad ties all day." Joe Stasiak in an effort to get his grandson to return to college told the boy, who'd quit school to work on the coal dock, "You wanted a paycheck, now you got it. Don't complain about the work." Ralph Slipkowski was like that with his sons. Ralph's life, Josie will tell you, hasn't been easy. He's wished for better, maybe a promotion to millwright. He's wanted the best for his boys. But there for a time when they wouldn't study, he'd had to lay down the law. "This is *my* house. You'll do as I say."

"So, Ralph," Josephine says, "if life isn't easy for the nuns at least they have a job and a place to live. Think of the years they've been here."

Ralph comes into the living room. "Is this tie on right?" he asks as Josie, in an effort to forestall her decline, primps before the mirror.

"Those neighborhood kids drive the nuns crazy. Yes, it is, Ralph, the tie is on straight. Right back to the Motherhouse, one right after another the nuns go. Lately it's worse."

Ralph rubs Butch Wax in his hair. After twenty-eight years, he still uses it. He still goes to Mass after twenty-eight years of marriage, too, but irregularly. Ralph and Josie had talked and talked before he let the boys attend St. Adalbert's school.

"It's my duty to give them a Catholic education," Josie had argued.

"Public schools are fine," Ralph had said, "but if your heart's set."

The boys are out of school now and gone, and the old-timers leaving, thinks Josie. *Their houses fall apart.* She thinks of how the city moves indigent families into vacant houses near the Slipkowskis' when public housing near the Fraser Shipyards is full. It's nothing intentional, she knows, nothing against Ralph and her, but at the moment most of the vacant houses are near theirs. Some of the Polish people have died, others gone away. The city purchases their houses for below market value, and in rush the newcomers. Now the children of strangers break glass on the sidewalks, roar down the alleys on motorcycles, and let their dogs loose in the streets. These people who put up the grease racks in the yard, Josephine has often wondered, where do they come from—far out in the country somewhere? Her husband thinks nothing of it. He doesn't worry too much about other people. He glances once more in the mirror, glances fearlessly at himself in the expensive mirror on his grandmother's dresser.

Josephine straightens her collar, sprays a reluctant curl with VO5. Ralph Slipkowski still putters around the room. *The boys are gone,* Josie thinks, *I'm getting older.* Was it so easy raising two children, keeping house, and staying out of debt when the flour mill was down or Ralph sick? she wonders. She recalls the struggle, like the time Ralph went to work for someone else and found he couldn't make it and had to return to the flour mill.

For the past few months, even a year now, the Sisters have been on Josie's mind the way mirrors have been on Ralph's. The nuns live in the neighborhood with newcomers who can't get into shipyard housing. Sister Stella, Sister Cecilia, and Sister Morris have come and gone. Their coifs were made of hard, starched cloth, wimples thrust from their neck. Their lacquered beads swung as they walked. Sister Bronisława has three new nuns to keep her company. The good sisters of *Skoła Wojciecha* care for Father Nowak's vestments, order votive candles, sweep the sacristy, lead the choir, teach, and pray. Before lunch, they pray several times.

Despite this, they are declining. Even the schoolchildren notice it. The children's own parents are losing the language. The neighborhood is failing. In the year the cornerstone was set, 1917, and after, students were more aware of their heritage, Josie thinks. Sister Bronisława they learned to fear and admire. The trainer of wayward Polish youth instructed them—she trained us, trained *me*, thinks Josie—to work, to honor the Polish flag, to grow up in the faith. Now the neighborhood's gone to hell with people of different faith, or of no faith. "People without a heritage who draw public assistance have overtaken us, Ralph," she says to her husband.

He's looking in the bedroom mirror. Fearing nothing, he moves from mirror to mirror, room to room, good mirrors, bad mirrors. In the expensive mirror on his grandmother's dresser, the one in the bedroom, he can see himself reflected better. In fact, it's such a good mirror that he can almost see the past in it. His own past has never troubled him much.

"Ralph Slipkowski!" she calls.

He appears with a flourish. "Yes, I'm ready," he says. His hair is gray. It stands up with Butch Wax. The gray matches his tweed jacket. "It begins at 7:30, doesn't it?" he asks. His face beams with goodwill. "Let's say goodbye to the old girl." He jiggles the car keys. He helps Josephine with her coat. It is early winter in Josie Slipkowski's soul. What's coming will be worse, she thinks. She doubts she can survive it. Extinction might be better, she tells herself.

"We've done okay, Ralph, haven't we?"

In the car, she thinks of Sister Bronisława. For a moment, she doesn't know who she's talking to, like the good Sister is there with them.

"How quickly time flies," Josie says.

She hears Ralph's chuckle.

"What?" he asks.

"I was dreaming of Sister. Are you listening, Ralph? It's okay if you don't."

I understand you, Ralph, my dear. Content with himself, he drives on. *You've done much good for the nuns and Father. Our sons are grown and gone away. And if you don't listen to me all the time now what does it matter? For twenty-eight years, you've listened. It's just that I don't know what our future holds. We're losing. I'm certain the strength of our family, our generation, is slipping away. Our boys, Warren and Terry, won't have the strength the Sisters brought with them from the old country. We are in decline, Ralph Slipkowski, and I am afraid.*

Ralph checks the rear-view mirror. He signals, turns up East 5th Street. He goes by the East End library, Peters' grocery store.

You're a harmless, good man whose shortcomings are modest ones. You, Warren, and Terry never shared the old customs with me. Sometimes I fear for myself. It was an odd, holy house I grew up in. Blessed candles lay in the drawers and Holy Water in different rooms. Black crepe on the door signaled death. If we dropped bread, Grandma made us kiss it. History haunts me. You and the boys don't know how bad. Now we must look over our shoulders and lock our doors when we leave the house.

Humming, Ralph drives effortlessly. He passes the Northern Block apartments. He turns one block down at the intersection by the drugstore and the bank.

Looking out the window, Josephine sees Mrs. Pawlikowski and Mrs. Fronckiewicz walking arm in arm. They are going the way of the Slipkowskis. They wave. Ralph pulls onto 4th Street.

"Those old ones—" he says about the two women.

But Josephine does not dismiss them so easily, for on winter mornings, these same old people, Mrs. Cieslicki, Mrs. Kiszewski, are here worshipping in the church of Polish immigrants. They come to Mass in bitter weather, the Sisters and the elderly. Nothing keeps them away. Why do old, weary people walk to a cold church where sometimes visiting priests say Mass at 6 A.M.? Over the years, Josie Slipkowski has justified her own faith through the faith of others. She has realized that out of all the old ones, including her own grandmother, out of all the immigrants from Poznań and Szczecin, Łomza and Białystok, at least one of them had more than simple ignorant faith to come each morning in prayer. One of them must have known something. This person—a peasant from Łódź, a baker from Katowice, a coachman from Zielona Góra—must have had a reason to think that getting up to pray was going to be worth it. What the old ones have is faith that has traveled far, thinks Josie.

SKOŁA WOJCIECHA STANDS AT 3rd Street and 22nd Avenue. From there you can see Fredericka Flour, where Ralph Slipkowski worked all his days, the oil dock, Hog Island, the Left-Handed River. Father rings the church bell. Ralph pulls up before Mrs. Konchak's garage. She waves her red kerchief. "You park here," she says. "It's okay."

Downstairs, you can smell coffee and flowers, cigarette smoke and baked goods. You can hear the roar of parish voices punctuated by laughter and song. Mr. Adam Burbul, Mrs. Tomaszewski, Augie and Louie Fronckiewicz and their mother and sisters, good, patient Helen Stromko from the dime store, the Nicoskis, Mrs. Cieslicki, Mrs. Podgorak—they have all assembled this Thursday evening. How Josephine Slipkowski wishes Warren and Terry, who went here eight years and played basketball in this hall, could see it, and her grandmother and grandfather, *Babusia* and *Dziaduś*, who are dead.

A classmate from 1934, a red-and-white carnation in his lapel, stands by the door. Ralph finds Josephine a chair. Father Nowak appears soon after the church bell has stopped ringing. On stage sits Sister Bronisława. The parishioners sing, *"Jeszcze Polska Nie Zginęła."*

How we're losing, thinks Josephine Slipkowski. *Except for their years at Szoła Wojciecha, what will distinguish the young who change their names and move away? Beyond St. Adalbert's, what remains? Beyond the nuns—?* Josephine recalls her mother telling her how, in the old times, Sister Bronisława went door to door to houses under quarantine. A purple card placed on the door by the Health Department meant typhoid, a red card, scarlet fever. Sister Bronisława would inquire, "Do you need food, Mrs. Pomerinski? Wood for your stove?" She was never weak, Josie thinks.

The gym's beige and green paint has faded and chipped; the hardwood floor is warped. Steam pipes run along the walls. The Rosary Sodality has decorated them with red and white bunting. All the old parishioners are here.

"The old people won't be with us much longer," Josephine

says to Ralph. Sister herself has been here a half-century, thinks Josie. "Maybe not a week or a month, Ralph, and we'll read in the news that all of them have finally gone away."

Some of the old ones speak no English. Those who do sing "Joining Poland's Sons and Daughter, We'll be Poles Forever" before Father Nowak clears his throat. Except for his voice, the hall is quiet.

"Tonight is an honor," he says. "We're here to give you this tribute, Sister Bronisława."

Settling her hands on her lap, Sister leans forward. She gazes at Father Nowak and down at the parishioners in the gym. She holds their gift, a little unsteadily—a red box with a white bow around it. Is it a scapular ... a book of the lives of the saints wrapped in the colors of Poland? Josie wonders. Sister Bronisława clasps it to her as she looks out at the walls she has known so long and at the people: a priest, a former novitiate, a grocer, and a newsman, a teacher and a banker and a Great Northern switchman, a worker in the drugstore, a street cleaner. Sister clutches the gift to the crucifix hanging from a gold chain around her neck. The parishioners' love goes with her.

"This," she says, "what's this?"

They stand to applaud.

Father Nowak reads a letter of good wishes. As others praise Sister Bronisława, Sister Benitia plays "God, Who Held Poland" on the piano. The old hall rings with haunted melodies that hurt a person with their sadness, the unforgotten music of the past. How can you describe the music? Chopin Paderewski ... It is something romantic.

The outsiders arrive the way they've been coming for centuries. Just as Sister and the others sing *"Jeszcze Polska,"* they hear the slow, airy settling of the door. Having seen lights, no doubt the newcomers figured on shooting baskets in the gymnasium. The old people, as they prepare to be invaded, hear them chattering, snapping their gum, bouncing the ball. Except for an occasional cough and some scraping of chairs, the hall is quiet. Even Father Nowak with the Bishop's letter tucked away in his jacket and Sister Bronisława in her chair on the stage turn to the entrance at the bottom of the stairs, anticipating the noise, the violent entry into their lives.

The two boys, defiant in torn jackets, walk in as though they have every right to be here. The children of strangers, they have invaded the neighborhood. They come and go freely. As the young ones roam the alleys, their older brothers accost the meek and humble.

When they see the old Polish people, the two boys stop. Hunched over, chewing their gum, they stare at the face of Poland. The country's age and civility mean nothing to them. One boy is pasty looking. Dark circles ring his eyes. The other, having tried growing a moustache, has succeeded in raising a few stringy hairs on the upper lip. Not over thirteen or fourteen, the two boys waver there. They do not attend this school. Perhaps they've never been in its gym. Or perhaps, having found Mr. and Mrs. Novozinski, Albert Roubel, the Stefankos, and one hundred others, the boys have discovered Mrs. Josephine Slipkowski's "verge of time" and can't break free again to darkness and the night yet. In finding the old people, they've found the past. It catches their imagination.

On the western front in 1939, Polish horse soldiers, their drawn swords raised and gleaming, charged German armored tanks. Defiantly, quixotically, soldiers from another century charged into the mechanical age and disappeared in the smoke. At the same time in Poland, young airmen practiced maneuvers in glider planes—not motorized airplanes like the enemy had, but glider planes. When Poland was finally lost to the enemy, the Polish State Radio broadcast a Polonaise and fell silent. The radio went off the air with something for dreamers.

Now in the gymnasium of the Polish school, it is as if,

through some stroke of fate, two intruders have discovered a forest clearing from which to observe horse soldiers gearing for the last, violent, fatal charge. In their one brief moment, the two witness for the first time their neighbors' nobility. It is evident in how the old people have turned out to honor the nun, in how they've kept up their traditions, their faith. While it has taken Josephine some months of constant doubting to observe, then to accept the newcomers' disregard for others, these children of strangers have taken only a minute to learn about centuries of struggle and grow bored. Wearying of the moment, the boys no longer appear to care what has been discovered this night. You could give them Sobieski charging the Turks, thinks Josie, Dąbrowski praying in his tent for a safe return from Italy, the Black Madonna pierced in the side and crying, Unrug at the Battle of Hel. You could give them Tadeusz Kościuszko freeing Warsaw from the Russians in the Spring of 1794, and the two intruders wouldn't care. These things resonate in the air about them. They lie in the mirrors in the Polish homes and in the wrinkles of the old faces and in the eyes and deep within the memory.

"What they staring at us for?" the boy with the circles under his eyes asks his friend. They bounce the ball, spy the table with the food and cake for Sister Bronisława. The other intruder spits out his gum, puts up a shot. The basketball, falling through, rips the paper decorations hanging from the net. It is a long, hopeless, ugly moment as they saunter to the table laden with hot dishes, hams, cheese, pickles, the large white cake.

"I'm not standing in line," the boy with the moustache says.

"Why should we?" the other says. Tossing the ball against the wall, he catches it, hands it to his partner, who throws it up again.

"They'll be gone," Josie whispers to Ralph. "Then there'll be a Polonaise."

But Ralph is not looking on the bright side. The intruders walk past Stella Nowatski, Mr. Mrozynski, Mr. Mackiewicz, Mrs. Kosmatka. When they pass him, the smirking boys do not look at Ralph, but *through* him as though he counts for nothing at all on this earth. That's when he has a vision of the days to come. Looking at the other parishioners' faces, for a moment he can't see his own face reflected, not in their glasses, not in their eyes, not in their Polish words. Suddenly nothing reflects Ralph Slipkowski of Superior, Wisconsin. It's not his wife's but his thinking about the future that changes now. More and more in the coming days, he sees in this vision of a world without depth, riots will be tearing cities apart, and presidents and dignitaries will be seized and put upon. It is not Josie's but Ralph Slipkowski's thinking that's changed. And now, of all things, he's suddenly becoming frightened of looking to the future.

Mrs. Burbul

Though everyone remarked how well the old woman looked, Mrs. Burbul would reply *"Nie szkodzi ... It doesn't matter"* and go her way through the fields surrounding the town. She went because the distances were very vast and wide and how you looked in God's eyes out there didn't matter. As she passed the houses at the edge of town, people would talk about the old woman, saying she looked healthy for her age and probably appeared this way to God in the fields, too.

Not many visited the fields the way the old woman did. In places, water lay across them, not draining because of the compact clay soil beneath. In fall and spring, grass fires burned, the smoke rising as through a wound in the earth. In the fields and wetlands surrounding the town, a few other people came to examine or to forget their lives. The soldier Vankiewicz, the Indian Gerald Bluebird whom Mrs. Burbul had seen shooting rabbits as a boy, a deaf-and-dumb man from across the Left-Handed River; each wandered out here to forget and be forgotten. The miles and miles of wetlands: no one thought much about them until a biologist came up to Superior from the state capitol to study the area.

For the old woman, his report had disturbing consequences. On three sides of town were rivers and on the fourth side Lake Superior; but now, he said, water lay deep in the ground, too. The biologist's report announced that below the town were both "subterranean springs" and eight-thousand-year-old water trying to seep down through the clay. With the droughts in states south of here, what could keep the government from draining away the water? She envisioned roads and fields becoming dust, pictured her soul withering as the water was drained. Over these wetlands, she'd prayed for years. Now she was so sick about what was happening that she could hardly eat.

"What do you want?" her daughter had asked that morning. "Oatmeal?"

"Soup."

"Soup again, Mama?"

Then the neighbor had come to increase her fears. "I want to show you more on this biologist's report," he'd said. The neighbor, Mr. Braiden, had been looking for articles on when to plant his broccoli and carrots when he spotted still another water report. "Look, water can't get down through our soil. That's what the report says in the morning paper. 'Flat terrain and clay soils around here make it an ideal place for wetlands.' Here, just look."

Mrs. Burbul didn't know about the weather or didn't care anymore when you planted a garden, but she knew the wetlands she walked over. Once before in her life, land and water planners had come. That time it was on foot and by armored vehicle and by plane, an entire country stolen. Now when she found it unnecessary to examine her conscience, when she was able to forget what they'd done fifty years ago to the old country, now there was much news again. Water planners were coming to drain the fields and sloughs—water which had helped Mrs. Burbul forget. She'd left her memories in the shallow water and treeless fields of the barren places hereabouts, and now things were changing.

At noon, her daughter went to the priest. Stanisława pulled the newspaper from her pocket. "Do you realize there's water down here, Father, maybe a couple of inches below us that, well … it's older than Christ?"

"How're things otherwise?" he asked, not seeming interested.

"Fine, but the water—"

"Good," said the priest, who lived in a dry area of town and had shallow thoughts. The Bishop had assigned him to the parish when the Polish priest, Father Nowak, died. The first thing Father O'Donnell did was remove the signs that read "Polish confessions heard this side" from the confessionals. "We speak American," he'd said. "But believe me," he was telling Stanisława, "she's on firm ground, your old mother. You tell her that." Pulling out the little phrase book, *Say It In Polish*, he tried to tell Stanisława to say "Diving is Prohibited," then he gave up.

"Give her this holy water," the priest said. "Tell her it'll make her feel better. Tell her ..."

Father O'Donnell laughed, but when Stanisława returned home the old woman, *Pani* Burbul, had packed a cardboard box with statuettes of Holy Mary and the painting of the Black Madonna of Częstochowa. She had her scarf and the heavy blue coat and was at the edge of the bed wondering, she told the daughter, whether it would offend God to also hang a scapular from her neck before she left.

"Ma, this is Superior, Wisconsin."

"I want to leave," she said to the daughter.

"The river's full of ice. It may be spring break up soon. Let's sit awhile. I've been to see the priest."

"I'm in a hurry," Mrs. Burbul said. She had the pockets of her coat full of little glass vials of holy water. The spiritual exercise was good for her, thought Stanisława, who'd seen her mother do this before and loved her very dearly but who wasn't interested in watching her pour holy water over the fields again. "What a curious custom," she'd been telling her husband for years when the old woman walked into the country where the river came from. Mrs. Burbul knew the lowlands and the river floodplain. Thankful to God and to Holy Mary, for fifty years she'd blessed the water in the fields of forgetfulness. "O God," her daughter would hear her say as though her mother's heart were breaking. Then Mrs. Burbul would spread over the bogs and sedge meadows the holy water the priest had blessed. Now the news that it was older, deeper water in the clay soil than anyone knew made her lose direction.

The scarf the daughter'd gotten her, the dull brown color of March, covered the old woman's forehead. She had it knotted beneath the chin. She'd buttoned the winter coat and stared out the window.

"Look, you don't have on your boots. It's cold," said the daughter. "How can you walk?"

The river was choked with ice. Over the trestle, which ran a half-mile across the floodplain, they watched the deaf-and-dumb man who worked at Fredericka Mill. They set their clocks by him. He'd come from the old country, had lost a brother there just as Mrs. Burbul had lost a father.

"Look, I see Borzynski going to work across the trestle. He's an old *dziaduś*. How much longer can he keep on?" Stanisława said.

Mrs. Burbul was crying, though. How could her daughter know what she, such an old woman, had left behind? In a while Stanisława rocked her mother back and forth and heard in the hours before the spring dusk old stories about a pail, a duck, and a goose. Then the old woman was silent.

"I'M HOME," STANISŁAWA's husband called later.

"We're here."

"What're you doing?" he asked when he came up. When he'd been drinking, he was good-natured and silly.

"I wouldn't joke about this. Ma thinks she's leaving us."

"Give her the car," he said.

"Mama," said the daughter. "This is your home. Why would you want to go?"

"Jesus, people are gonna say we went bad if they see her

walking around in the cold without boots on. *Babusia*," he said. It was the only Polish word he knew. "Where're you heading? I'll take you to the butcher's shop to buy you your supper if that's where you want to go."

Mrs. Burbul pulled out a handful of tissues and a rosary from her coat.

"Come, Ma. Finish your soup. I'll heat it up," Stanisława said. Downstairs, she hung her mother's coat. "You can wear it again tomorrow." At supper, the old woman prayed as the daughter prepared the meal. As such times with her mother far away in prayer, Stanisława would stroke her hair or pat the old woman's hands.

"These water plans they've got going," Larry was telling them both, "they're going to drain everything in sight ... that's what the word is. It's going to mean the rebirth of our city, a new age from old water. They're draining us dry. I've got things to do around here to get ready for the future," he said, getting up from the table.

"*Idź z Bogiem,*" the old woman said. "God be with you." Finishing her beetroot soup, she went up to her room before Mr. Braiden could come to upset her more. All over, she knew, were men like the neighbor and her son-in-law who tried to change the sky you walked beneath. She saw them in the shadows the moon cast on the walls in her room. If you looked up, the men would be staring down into the earth as if to bury you. If you looked down, they'd say you had too much on your mind, that you shouldn't be thinking so much. "Look up!" Someday when Stanisława was old, when maybe she too had had things stolen from her, and Larry and the priest, then the daughter would walk by herself into the fields under the moon. But the memory of the old woman would be fading for her, Mrs. Burbul thought. Then maybe the daughter would sleep fitfully for how she'd not understood the old woman, her mother Mrs. Burbul, when she was alive years ago.

"It's coming, the day's coming," Larry was saying. "It's necessary we share the wealth of water. Pure, clean water from Lake Superior and the wetlands. We're going to be famous. They're studying us close. We got all the water up here they need in Kansas and other dry places."

The more the neighbor and son-in-law talked, the more they confused swamps with sedge meadows, the more Mrs. Burbul, who heard their voices up through the vent, feared the land would come to dust. It was like before with the invaders. That time it was Nazis, the Communists. Now the land would be lost again. What hope was there for a son-in-law like this? she thought. Both the son-in-law and the neighbor were fools who hollered all the time. She could hear them—or was it the priest she heard hollering? He'd also come to the house for a drink.

"When I got home, I tell you, Father O'Donnell, she'd packed her dresses in a sack," Stanisława was saying to him as she led the priest upstairs. "It's like this water beneath gets older. And she didn't have on boots, like she wants to freeze."

"I don't know," said Father O'Donnell. "I could look in the phrase book to try to get through to her. But it's like these old ones, they're different. They've got things on their mind they just won't talk about. How deep do you have to go to reach them, I wonder?"

Sitting by the bed, he said, "Isn't it cold today, Grandmother? What a wonderful woman you are." Then he read to her: "'Save me, O God, for the waters threaten my life. I am stuck in the abysmal swamp where there is no foothold; I have reached the watery depths; the flood overwhelms me.'"

WHEN THE DAUGHTER, promising to be right back, brought the priest downstairs, the old woman blessed the corners of the room. *"O jakie to szczęscie, ż Cię, o Boże,"* she prayed before she lay down to dream of water. You never knew how deep the water was. Odra, Czernia, Pliszka, Postemia: these were the lakes and rivers she remembered from the old country, the farm of her brother, how she'd brought water and straw for "Kartuz," the horse. Hearing Stanisława again, she said, "Plotters and schemers they all come. They shoot these goose on our farm. Then they ask for my father's pail. 'This pail is no good to water horses.'"

"I know, Ma. You've told it all before."

"They take us into camp. They throw coal and wood at us when we're tired from working. The cook, he was Polish man, fixed us horsemeat, called us 'swinia, filthy pig' even though he was one of us. Everyone in camp is dying. When the guards run off after the war end, we pulled him down, kick him. 'We geeve you Polish swine,' we said."

THE PRIEST, DRINKING with Larry and Mr. Braiden, heard none of this. The deeper you went in the waters of memory, the colder they became, thought Mrs. Burbul. The cook's skin … the blade of a shovel in his skull was like the blade of a shovel draining the earth. The water would be funneled to deserts in Kansas, United States. She was sure the water dreamer next door had told her this.

"WHAT IN HELL? WE HAVEN'T got a pail for her horse," Larry said when he and his wife came up after the party in the kitchen. "This is Superior, Wisconsin."

"She's been talking."

The old woman heard them at the top of the stairs. The floodplain of the Left-Handed River would be dark, the long, wide river so full of ice that led you up into the land where the compass lay.

He had taken off his clothes. He had made her do it, too. The prisoners had scattered. She'd stolen from the cook's filthy pockets the eye of a potato. She'd stolen the compass she'd later buried here in America where the Left-Handed River runs. God forgive me, she thought.

He geeve potato… rutabaga. He geeve me the best of the rotten horsemeat for food.

THOUGH IT WAS ALMOST spring, nothing was alive in America except the river under the trestle, which had started to shoot water up from beneath the rotting ice, streams of water. Larry and the daughter had taken her there one day. Ice was a land you couldn't get over, Mrs. Burbul thought. The ice on the Left-Handed River came down toward the lake from where a stolen compass still lay after fifty years. She had once walked far up the river ice into the forest. Along its length, the long white river now moved as they watched it, and the whole earth had seemed to move in one direction *and you were naked and his face was cold when he was through. And all for a potato or a bowl of the horsemeat soup.*

As Mrs. Burbul's daughter lay in bed remembering Larry saying, "Jesus, look at the river starting to break up," the old woman walked quietly in the hall between the rooms, having lost her way again.

"Mama, your pot's in your room. You don't have to go downstairs to the bathroom. Why are you sitting up so late?" Mrs. Burbul heard the daughter saying.

"Nie szkodzi … it doesn't matter. Go to sleep," she said. *Up through the furnace vent, she'd heard them all night arguing the serious nature of bogs and rivers.* The old woman, who'd given part of her confession to the priest, heard the water dreamers' arguments. The priest had joined in to argue about God. She could confess, but not to him, not to the new priest, how they'd beaten the cook. The priest, drunk, was arguing that there was no God.

The bleeding, half-dead cook had seen her coming. She'd wanted to take back something for what he'd stolen from her. There was a compass pointing west. She could feel his dirty legs through the pockets where the compass was. The others had run off. She was spitting on him. She'd pulled the hair from the cook's head. The shovel... "Bless me, Father, for I have sinned," she was saying in Polish, words which neither Stanisława nor the priest would ever find in a phrase book for modern readers. "Do you want me to sit in your room with you for a while?" the daughter asked Mrs. Burbul when the old woman had come up for the night earlier.

But now the house was quiet, drained of sound. Sitting on the bed, Mrs. Burbul could dream of how life had once been in the old country before she'd come to America. Everyone else was dreaming of their future—the priest, Mr. Braiden, Larry, her son-in-law. They were going east, west, south, everywhere in America, but she, directionless, was sitting here alone in the room. There were lines like lines of soldiers along her wall where the moon shone in. That was how life came and went in the fields of America, like long columns of invading soldiers that each night from all directions came after her into the house with the moon.

THE PRESIDENT OF THE PAST

You may join our Polish Club if you are "an upright descendant of the Slavic race." If you are older than forty-five but of Slavic heritage, you must settle for "social membership status," in which case you can't hold office, vote on lodge matters, or receive sickness or death benefits; however, our by-laws state that social members can attend "all social doings on the society level." Our one social doing is a semiannual lunch of cabbage rolls, sausage, dark bread, and beer. In the late 1940s and throughout the 1950s when I accompanied my father "Buck" Mrozek to the club, things were different. The lodge hosted casino nights, dances, dinners, picnics. The bar was full even with no special events scheduled.

The son of the accordion player "Buck" Mrozek, I joined the club in middle age. After living in the Buffalo suburbs, the prospect of better employment drew me back. I paid the $6 membership fee and the $22 year's dues and was sworn in at Superior's Polish Club. A few years later, with no one willing to take over, I became president. At monthly meetings, I gain a sense of connectedness to something remembered and missed from the men who keep me in office.

One evening in the bar I heard how Joseph Smiegel rode a white horse in city parades years before. At home I have a photograph of him in uniform with the *Gwardyo Pułaskiego*, the Pulaski Guard—a ceremonial military society founded in 1902. On leather helmets, *rogatywka*, an eagle rises above polished visors. Rising from the crown of the helmet, a pike holds a square leather top from which feathered plumes fall to tunic collars. Epaulets decorate the men's shoulders, and braids run across the coat fronts. With sword drawn, *Kapitan* Smiegel stands before his men. Our display case holds his helmet and sash.

In the case in a corner of the bar also lies a medallion attached to a long, red ribbon. Printed on the medallion is *CZŁONEK*, "member," and on the ribbon with the delicately spun gold border: *TOWARZYSTWO ŚŚ PIOTRA i PAWŁA 1903*, meaning "Society of Saints Peter and Paul 1903." Beside it hangs a black and silver ribbon that gives the date when, and place where, the lodge was founded:

TOWARZYSTWO
Tadeusz Kościuszko
Zal. Dnia 1-go Sierpnia
1928 ROKU
w SUPERIOR, WIS.

To go with this, we have a photo of an old wooden church. Mourners surround a casket whose half-open lid exposes the head and shoulders of a deceased man. Two lines of pallbearers and mourners in long winter coats and wearing Kosciuszko ribbons extend to the foreground in the photo: bare trees, snow, everyone staring at the photographer except the dead man, a lodge member who, at the center of the occasion in his honor, is left out. I don't recognize the living or the dead, but know them to be former lodge members by the ribbons on their coats and know they must not be forgotten.

Now when I pound the gavel and say, "The monthly meeting of the Thaddeus Kosciuszko Fraternal Aid Society is called to order," I look out at twenty or fewer ribbonless lodge brothers sitting on ragged chairs in a room above a bar. Fifty years ago there would have been four times that many members present. We hear an opening prayer, minutes of the previous meeting, a "Report of the Guardian of the Sick," and other agenda items before a closing prayer read by Frank Stepan, the vice president. Alone in the room after the members have gone downstairs for a beer, I try to remember what has gone on.

I WILL PROBABLY BE the last president of the Polish lodge. The history of presidents will go from an accordion player's and violin player's son (my mother performed for Calvin Coolidge when he had his "Summer White House" in Superior), all the way back to the men in the black coats in the funeral picture ... back even to *Kapitan Smigiel* on the white horse.

This may happen very soon. The $22,000 in debts trouble us. Though the sign outside reads "PUBLIC WELCOME," few non-members drop by to sit in the bar. The Polish National Anthem has been replaced on the jukebox by a Frank Sinatra song. On some days, no one at all stops in at our club.

Two businessmen would like to turn it into an "interactive sports bar." A Finn and a German, they promise that if we sell to them and if the room upstairs isn't reserved we can use it for monthly meetings and we can have a storage closet. But what about the *rogatywka*, sword, and sash in the glass case downstairs in the bar, or Mr. Gapa's 1914 account book in the office showing whom he loaned money to so they could bring relatives here from the Old Country? These things would have to go in storage. With our past stored away, the club could disappear like Superior's Polish and Slovak churches. Churches gone, lodge membership dwindling, old people gone. If it keeps up, we'll have no memories. They'll all be in storage.

In the 1950s when the club was in a building a few blocks away, when the grain mills and "the World's Largest Ore Docks" on Superior's waterfront were enjoying their best shipping seasons, and when, all in all, the world was a little younger, church, Polish Club, and neighborhood were more important to people. My father played the accordion. I hear him in memory. Within earshot of his polkas in the East End lived my paternal grandparents, Antoni and Mary Mrozek, my aunts Ann Novack and Cecilia Simzek, and my two great aunts who, never married, took care of my great-grandfather Andrzej who played obereks on the concertina.

My mother was also a musician. She was daydreaming one day as she practiced. My sister was out somewhere; my father was working at the flour mill. Just my mother and I sat in a sunlit kitchen, a vase of lilacs between us.

"I want to tell you about the Black Madonna, Our Lady of Częstochowa," she said. As she put down the violin, she stared out the window at the warm May morning. "Centuries ago the Swedes invaded Poland."

"What happened then?"

"They almost conquered Poland except for this monastery at *Jasna Góra* where the Swedes saw a beautiful picture and attempted to pull it from the wall. But the Madonna's picture wouldn't budge. When a soldier cut Her face, others looked up to see the Blessed Madonna bleed from Her wound. Seeing this, the men fell to their knees, then fled. Then all the invaders withdrew, and Poland was saved."

That morning I wondered whether my mother missed her own mother who'd told her the legend of the Madonna. Perhaps it was my mother's violin playing that made her recall the story for me. Grandmother Rowinska, my maternal grandmother, lived one-and-a-half miles away in another part of the East End. We didn't see her quite as often as other relatives who lived closer because my father worked long hours, and my mother couldn't drive a car and was busy with my sister and me. Mother could dream, however.

On the day she told me about the Black Madonna, I think she missed her mother and the Old Country. My mother had been playing "Dreamer's Waltz ... *O Młynarce z Pewnej Wsi Walc.*" In fact, my mother's side of the family was more the dreamers, the romantics, it seemed to me; my father's side was more practical. Was this the year the apple tree showered and blessed us with its blossoms one Sunday after Mass when Mother set a table outside for breakfast? Our peonies bloomed around the time the apple tree did. Pink apple blossoms would be clinging to the wire stand supporting the peonies. Soon delicate white lilacs would come out, then orange poppies. She'd daydream like she did on the morning of my history lesson, then play the violin with orange flowers for her backdrop. The way she told me the legend of Our Lady seemed like a dream— a personal, maternal introduction of a son to ancestral custom. I thank her for this. And during this time in the evening after work, Buck Mrozek, composer of the famous "East End Polka" and my father, practiced his accordion, so he, too, could dream. I bless and thank both parents for their lessons.

Now I think of the club and of my family as I whisper prayers. I don't want to let the club go to a German and a Finn because the few active members who remain know our ancestors met during these very same summer and winter hours as we do, read the same opening prayer at meetings, and followed the same order of business; "the Report on Members Whose Suspensions Have Been Lifted," "the Report of the Guardian of the Sick ..." The Polish and American flags stood before them as they do before us. How can we let this go? How can I myself let the club go? Almost everything is in storage. Yet in the faded map of Poland on the wall, in the display case, in the flag that needs washing, and in the stale air of the Polish Club, I still have a place to come to where I can cherish my heritage.

When Mr. Kubos, our sergeant-at-arms, isn't well and I, president, have to prepare the upstairs room for the meeting, I don't say much, realizing it is a job I must do. I live in a Pulaski Room of memories and write them over and over as though I were practicing a musical instrument, say a violin that is playing "Dream Waltz" or an accordion playing "East End Polka." When during the course of a lodge meeting, I ask, "Are there any new members?", no one says anything in the Pulaski Room. No one joins the Society. I myself don't talk much afterwards either, just have a beer to forget where we are heading. I don't want to leave the hall. I don't want the hall's memories to go. I'm afraid of what will happen when they do. I, Rick Mrozek, am president of the past.

WHEN YOU WALK OUTSIDE AFTER a meeting, after the closing prayer and the beer, when you walk out and the same gray, winter sky meets you that met other worthy lodge brothers for over seventy years ... that met Smigiel and The Guard, you see a block south of here one of Superior's passenger train depots, closed now. Look the opposite way north two blocks into the hard wind stinging your eyes and whipping the Polish flag and you see where the first club stood that meant so much to others and to me when I went there as a child with my father. There is a story about the closing of the old, rickety building. When the pounding feet of polka dancers weakened the foundation, the fire marshal said he'd have to close the Polish Club because the foundation was giving way under the heavy pounding of the feet. How could you make dancers stop when the air was blue with smoke or when the beer flowed or when the accordion player, fingering his keys, promised "Pennsylvania Polka" or my father's "East End Polka"?

When the building *was* condemned (too much dancing finally), the Thaddeus Kosciuszko Lodge, the Polish Club, bought the new hall, where I am president. This was so long ago: 1963. Here at the new clubrooms, the membership thought there'd be no problems with "sympathetic vibrations," the engineering term for what occurred at the old club. The new brick building with the flags out front looked like a pill-box. The bar portion lay below ground. Diesels shunting boxcars in the nearby freightyards couldn't shake these walls. Two dozen accordion-playing lodge members, my father among them, couldn't shake unshakable walls.

If, after the meetings in the unshakable building these days, feeling slightly shaken you drive past the shipyards, you still see ore boats laid up for winter repairs. At the elevators, grain still rots in wet, stinking piles. Along Belknap Street, if you go home that way toward East End, the storefronts are run-down as they were in 1928. Little has been done to beautify Superior since *Kapitan* Smigiel appeared on a white horse.

Years ago my uncles Augie and Louie, my mother's brothers, would have returned from lodge meetings this way, down Belknap to their parents', my maternal grandparents', house. My maternal grandfather, Wincenty Rozinski, would have come home this way, too. His dreaming grandson, I, Rick Mrozek, drive home past their house on the way to my own. Now I wonder where I have come to at age 58, into what strange dream of old neighborhoods where no relatives live anymore.

My dreaming grandmother who left Poland when she was fourteen—and whom my dreaming mother missed so terribly that she played the violin to think of her—my grandmother and grandfather Wincenty built their East End home near the Northern Pacific railroad tracks. Grandmother would have heard trains passing north then west to Duluth and passenger trains heading east to Ashland, Wisconsin, or to Ewen and Marquette, Michigan. I wonder whether eighty years ago with my grandfather at the flour mill, Grandmother, alone in her kitchen with the sprig from the lilac bush in her hand, ever whispered to the passing trains, "Where have I come to?" as she looked out at the empty fields and at the trains that might bring Polish people to Superior. Quiet and gentle like my mother, she spoke little in either language except when she was dreaming.

Now I try to speak her language, the old peoples' language, when I say, "*Babusia*, are you there in the kitchen window? It is eighty years ago. Is Grandfather Wincenty gone to work at the flour mill? Is Mother at a violin lesson? Is the Black Madonna's picture hanging on the wall?" In my grandmother's back yard if I could again go there as a child, I would pass the rain barrel beside the barn, pass Augie's garden, pass Louie's goldfish pond where the gladioli were cleared back beneath the apple tree. That's where I'd look for my maternal grandmother, the dreamer with her lilac spring. This is the place I'd look for memories of all my ancestors. Maybe now—having seen parents and grandparents die in the East End and my great-aunts Helcha and Fronia and uncles *Władziu*, Louie, and Augie die—maybe now at my age and as president of a Polish lodge that is declining, I could get from them the answers I seek to make this remembering easier.

I am a president of the past, calling the meeting of ghosts to order.